T0083444

Dispatches from Moments of Calm

THE
SEAGULL
LIBRARY OF
GERMAN
LITERATURE

ALEXANDER KLUGE

89 stories

Dispatches from Moments of Calm

GERHARD RICHTER

64 pictures

TRANSLATED BY NATHANIEL MCBRIDE

LONDON NEW YORK CALCUTTA

The translator would like to thank the Europäisches Übersetzer-Kollegium in Straelen, north-west Germany, for their support in the translation of this book.

This publication was supported by a grant from the Goethe-Institut India

Seagull Books, 2019

Originally published as Alexander Kluge / Gerhard Richter, *Nachrichten von ruhigen Momenten. 89 Geschichten. 64 Bilder.*

First published in English translation by Seagull Books, 2016

Additional work by Thomas Combrink

ISBN 978 0 8574 2 702 1

British Library Cataloguing-in-Publication Data
A catalogue record for this book is available from the British Library
Typeset by Seagull Books, Calcutta, India
Printed and bound by WordsWorth India, New Delhi, India

1

These were some of the things he wanted to remember: the plants with their strict yellow blossoms, the red southern colours among the bushes. His daughter shifting from one foot to the other, clearly impatient. His son immersed in his schoolbooks, swotting away.

As the weekend flew past, he was eager to speak to someone about his impressions of it. But what came into his head weren't sentences. He resolved to 'remember' everything so he could find the words for it *later*. Where should he put these images? Which part of the mind is responsible for remembering images? It is not a 'value' that can be repeated. Clouds protected the house and the garden from the unrelenting sun. A storm was expected that evening. Only two days earlier, in another place entirely, white blossoms, like the ones described in *The Man without Qualities*, were swaying above the concrete-covered yard and rubbish bins of the town hall. Unpoetically located blossoms. This too was a chance occurrence that he did not expect to experience a second time in his life.

❊ ❊ ❊

The blue tit, a habitué of smart hotels whose courage had never truly been tested by the guests on the terrace, approached the cup of cappuccino with its gaze firmly fixed on the biscuit, twice the size of a two-euro coin, that lay next to its saucer. The bird's delicate feet were barely able to gain a hold on the glass tabletop. The rush matting beneath the glass gave it the appearance of a surface it did not really have. The blue tit 'smelt' the sugary confection with its eyes. It knew the value of this particular piece of loot, precisely assessing it despite the fact that it could only be carried off in crumb-sized pieces. The delicacy's yellow colour could not be mistaken for anything else.

It approached the object twice before pecking at it. Its beak could gain no purchase on the large biscuit. The blue tit flew off, and it was some time before, with great vigilance, it approached the desirable item again. It was a pretty animal—so pretty that one could imagine it stuffed, the pride and joy of an eighteenth-century ornithological institute— assuming, that is, it wasn't considered too commonplace a specimen to form part of a collection. There were no Enlightenment thinkers on the terrace, nor indeed anyone with any experience in catching a bird by hand, killing and stuffing it. Where in their homes would the people on the terrace have put such a splendid specimen?

In the meantime the animal had conducted several more experiments, and actually managed to shove the biscuit to the edge of the table by batting at it with its beak. Did the bird think it was possible to push the biscuit off the edge so it would break into pieces? None of the adults at the table imagined the bird was 'thinking' anything. Having briefly touched on this incident, the conversation turned to other subjects. Then, about eight minutes later, the blue tit seized the biscuit in its beak and flew several metres to a gravelled area bordering the terrace—and from there it (along with its prize) flew under a bush, from where, in turn, the biscuit would presumably be carried in pieces to a nest over the course of the afternoon and shared among its young. Never before had the bird made off with such an enormous store of provisions. It took 23 attempts to achieve a balance between the bird's small, airworthy body (whose delicate feet were indicative of its frailty), its greed and the object's substantial weight.

❅ ❅ ❅

Telephones shrilled in the offices above. Here, at the side of the road, were a couple of tumbleweeds. We ran down, planning on getting a shot of one of them. The chief editor wanted just such an informal shot of a tumbleweed.

—The camera's too high, Mr Lüring.

—It won't go any lower.

We took the camera off its tripod. Even on the ground, its lens was too high to get a shot of the tumbleweed. We had to dig a little hole in the narrow space between the sidewalk and the road, the place where dogs would come to relieve themselves. From this shallow depression the tumbleweed was clearly visible, as passing lorries shielded it against the light.

IT WAS A DETAIL. We needed the image as a cutaway shot so we could tone down a plot development that had acquired an exaggerated importance.

— Use the lens with the longer focal length, Mr Lüring. The movements on the road behind the tumbleweed need to appear blurred.

— You mean they should only be visible as shadows?

— As light, shadows and abundant grey tones, to emphasize the shot's importance.

❊ ❊ ❊

— We cannot hope to find any trace of the first 600 million years of our planet's existence.

— Why not?

— The matter was too hot. The bombardment from the accretion disc that surrounded the earth was too heavy. All trace of what happened has been erased. This is the so-called PRIMARY TURMOIL.

— And you're saying that this event never came to an end, that it's still continuing?

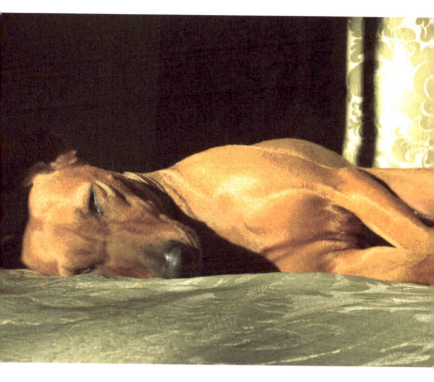

—Absolutely.

—With what consequences?

—That all the iron atoms in the nuclei of our cells are in a state of turmoil, in other words, that this turmoil is what we call life.

✾ ✾ ✾

The radio signal of the binary pulsar J 04374715 has a period of 5.757451831072007 milliseconds. In the course of a hundred thousand years, this celestial timepiece has altered by a millisecond at most. Endurance of quasi-stellar objects.

❊ ❊ ❊

In 1946, the Russian astrophysicist Gamov, transported in a US Air Force plane from California to Canada, from there to Washington, and from there to Florida, on each occasion to deliver a lecture, saw WITH HIS OWN EYES—while waiting in a noisy cafe on New York's Fifth Avenue during one of the few quiet moments he had to himself—the rotation of atoms and subatomic particles, their spin, the constant revolution of molecules and planets, the rapidly turning stars, galaxies and superclusters. This SNAPSHOT appeared to him as a uniform movement, divisible by the spin numbers one-and-a-half and one, similar to an extremely complex clock or a piece of music, like the one he'd heard in Venice Cathedral during a visit Stalin had allowed him to make there in the 1930s. On the back of the cafe bill he noted down this observation as a mathematical formula, which initially seemed no more than a visual aberration, like the movement of blood corpuscles in front of the pupil when one gets up too quickly with the sun in one's eyes. Later he was unable to read the scrawl he had quickly

jotted down. Never again did he see the world with such precision.

❆ ❆ ❆

Vain search by two pigeons for a moment of calm: their two plump bodies, distant descendants of Mediterranean rock pigeons, had sought each other out in this city in the middle of Europe. For weeks they'd been trying to build a nest. The spot they'd chosen for it was remarkably unsuitable—the steel surface in front of the sliding lift doors on the second floor of an office building. The lift ran up the side of the building, and the people using it had to tread on or sweep aside the twigs and grass stalks which, hastily gathered by the male, were the symbolic indication of a nest. Even the opening and closing of the lift's mechanical doors was enough to demolish it.

There were, as yet, no eggs in the nest. The male would often join his mate and position his chest next to hers. It seemed as if he were trying to nourish his companion with 'warmth'.

On this particular Friday evening, things were looking hopeful for the two prospective parents, since—though of course the pigeons could not have known this, having no notion of the days of the week—very few people would be using the lift over the weekend ahead. So it might at least be possible to start laying their eggs and incubating them. Let thereafter come what may: it is the evolutionary lot of pigeons to begin by procreating, even when the next steps in the process of propagating the species remain unforeseeable to them.

Thus they sat. A handleless broom, left there by the office staff on Thursday in the hope it might scare them off, appeared to them to be a shelter of sorts; a clump of bushes perhaps, or even an outcrop of rock. The wood

they'd gathered had made the surface of the steel tracks in front of the lift door look like a genuine nesting place.

Late on Sunday evening they could still be seen nesting there peacefully. Although too little time had passed for the decisive moment of egg-laying to arrive, and for the incubation of these valuable possessions to begin. Then, late on Monday morning, I saw the man from pigeon control. He and his assistant were lurking in the stairwell of the building, rod and net in hand. The pigeons appeared to have abandoned their nesting place. Pigeons are cautious animals who would almost certainly have spotted anyone reconnoitring their territory. The breeding pair had fled, and the pigeon catcher was working on how he could lure them back. He could have scattered their nest and slung up a net which would have stopped the pigeons from entering the space in front of the elevator door. Some of those watching, including the people using the building (office staff enjoying their breaks), found themselves emotionally engaged and became interested in the pigeons' determination to procreate. They translated it into human terms. At the same time, they wondered whether, instead of catching them in a net, it might not be easier for the pigeon catcher to poison or otherwise kill the pigeons. No, was the professional pigeon hunter's reply, I don't kill pigeons. I catch them, transport them a hundred kilometres out of the city, and set them free in the open. It's possible that they may be killed by birds of prey there, but I don't do it. I'm not a pigeon hunter either, but a specialist in pigeon *control*. I advise property owners and companies on how they can protect their buildings against the superior numbers of these powerful animals, and the disastrous, if not immediately visible, effects of their droppings. You see, he said, we've put pigeon sticks above the elevator here; they prevent pigeons from building their nests or roosting in the alcoves. So the pigeons' rather crazy idea was probably the result of successful pigeon control measures. There were few other places left in the building where it was possible to build a nest.

Not all the witnesses believed that the pigeon control officer would drive along a hundred kilometres of country roads to release the pigeons merely because regulations required it. For the moment his problem consisted in luring the prospective parents back to their nesting place so he could catch them. By late afternoon, there was no sign of either the catcher or the pigeons. The odd couple's opportunities were limited to the period between Friday evening and Monday morning, in other words, to the period of the Christian days of rest. In the future only those newly arrived Mediterranean rock pigeons who succeed in building their nest and laying and incubating their eggs in periods of time like this will have any chance of survival in our big cities. For the dove, the third animal of the Trinity, an evolutionary haste has become mandatory.

❊ ❊ ❊

He was young to be driving a mechanical digger. At New Year's he wanted to send a signal to his fiancée, who lived nearby, from the cab of his digger as it stood atop a hill in the middle of a building site. Three of his friends, who were to be groomsmen at his wedding, were ready to turn up at the appointed time.

Holger Fehling made careful preparations for everything, and one of the precautions he took this time was to test out his fireworks the day before. This meant that a doctor and ambulance would have immediately been on hand (something one couldn't have hoped for on New Year's Eve), and the rescue team and its vehicle would have quickly reached the hill where the digger stood (which also probably wouldn't have been possible on the last day of the year, because parked cars would have blocked the way to the building site). And Holger would have been saved, had there been anything of him left to save. He had prepared

three explosive devices. Two lay at his feet in the glass cabin that surmounted the digger he operated every day. These giant bangers consisted of aluminium cans he'd patched together himself and filled by hand with explosives taken from the building site's own arsenal—firecrackers the size of a melon. In one hand he held this creation, in the other a firework. Suddenly the device exploded. The shockwave tore the young driver's lungs to shreds. A farmer watching the scene from 500 yards away thought that the glass housing on top of the digger had caught fire. He telephoned the fire brigade. The young DIY enthusiast died on the way to the hospital. The next day, his fiancée and friends waited for hours for the promised signal from the top of the digger. The machine stood there silently. The four of them went looking for their friend. Eventually they asked at a police station and learnt of the accident.

❊ ❊ ❊

During an argument in the smokers' corner of a dance hall in Straubing on New Year's Eve, a stranger pressed a burning cigarette into the eye of a 20-year-old man and left without anyone else trying to stop him. Did it matter more to the people there that they call an ambulance or that they pursue the attacker? What, in practical terms, could the others have done to prevent the attack? Everyone in the group was shocked and frightened by the stranger's aggression. The young smoker did not regain his sight in the eye that had been attacked. The police have opened a criminal investigation.

❊ ❊ ❊

After delivering a lecture in Stockholm in 1908, Rudolf Steiner was asked what the term 'sense of chance' was supposed to mean. Steiner avoided the question. He rattled on about the concept of chance. What is a chance event? That which chances to happen to me. The bounty of nature and

the circumstances in which I live enrich my life. The opposite of chance—*Zufall* in German—would be *Abfall*, or defection. As when someone betrays me, when he defects (*abfällt*) from our common cause. As when I lose something I did not need to begin with.

In the summer of 2002, several children from the southern Russian city of Ufa, who had been awarded a holiday in Spain for their outstanding marks at school, missed their connecting flight after their plane arrived late at Moscow airport. All of them died miserably in the chartered aeroplane that was hired to take them to their final destination.

Shortly before they boarded the doomed aircraft, two servants of a government official in Ufa arrived to take his children off the flight. They refused to let the children onto a flight that had not originally been arranged for the journey, and took the disappointed youngsters back to Ufa, where the following day they were welcomed (the accident having occurred in the meantime) with open arms. This, an initiate of the science of anthroposophy confided, was a recent example of the theory of the sense of chance. What else could have caused the servants to remove the two children from the company of their ill-fated friends other than a sense of this kind?

How could they have had a presentiment of the danger lurking above the waters of a foreign country? The causalities constituting the spirit of this catastrophe had not yet converged. That's true, confided the anthroposophist, but the senses orientated towards such future chance events do not require any knowledge of them. They know of them in advance, not because they are able to trace their causes but because they 'see' densities that signal danger to those capable of recognizing them.

So do angels work with a sense of chance?

They don't work with one, but they have one.

❊ ❊ ❊

Snow on a copper roof. It belongs to a building that houses a state opera. The art form this building serves has existed since 1607. More than 400 years of opera. The opera impresario Schulz has worked out that there are 80,000 opera scores. He conjectured that, if they were all gathered together, they would form a single score, something like a CITY of music.

❈ ❈ ❈

Commitment to a colleague with a sore throat. In February 2013, the virulent lung infection that had been going about threw the programme of one of Germany's leading opera houses into utter disorder. The singer playing the title role in *Rigoletto* at Munich's Bavarian State Opera lay miserably stricken on his hotel bed, his chest covered in hot packs. There was no question of him singing. By one o'clock that afternoon, the singer playing Falstaff at Milan's opera house had been ordered to get in a car. He set off over the Alps for the Bavarian capital. Just a quarter of an hour before the orchestra began its general rehearsal, he was being shown his place in the wings by assistants. There remained seven minutes for discussions with the principal conductor. The substitute baritone from Milan sang his part so proficiently and 'with such tender strength' (opposite a Gilda who stood 20 metres away from him, who had to coordinate her movements with the dramaturg playing his part on stage, and whom he'd never met) that, following his monologue to the servile courtiers in the second act, the members of the orchestra drummed upon their instruments, an honour rarely shown to those performing at the opera house for the first time. Just 20 minutes after the moving end of the opera, the singer, who could sing 16 different parts from Verdi's operas, was put in his car and driven through the night back to Milan. The next morning at eleven o'clock the same baritone appeared for the dress rehearsal of *Falstaff* in the northern Italian capital.

❊ ❊ ❊

Total commitment. He was a singer who gave more than his all. Dramatic renunciation. He would forget to spare his own voice, with the result that during many performances he would become vocally bankrupt, capable only of still displaying technique. His voice was 'rough and gravelly, but possessed a solid and highly metallic core'. It would, wrote the critic of the *New York Times*, be difficult to surpass his *cri de coeur* of 'Ah, la maledizione' in *Rigoletto*. By contrast, the critic of the *Washington Post*, while acknowledging that the baritone's singing possessed a certain aplomb, declared it to be 'without any stylistic delicacy'. That wounded him deeply.

Leonard Warren, born Leonard Warenhoff in New York in 1911, took over the role of the Doge in *Simone Boccanegra* from the legendary Lawrence Tibbett. The part put him among the leading group of his generation in the world of baritones. He was UTTERLY UNSPARING of himself in defending the position he'd so strenuously sought while maintaining a reputation for being 'sensitive' and 'refined'. However, it was precisely this, the QUALITY OF FEELING of his singing, that was disputed. The critic at the *Washington Post* was willing to grant him only a certain NATURAL POWER.

March 4, 1960 was the opening night of Verdi's *La forza del destino* at the Metropolitan Opera House in New York. Leonard Warren sang the part of Don Carlos, brother to the unfortunate Leonora (Renata Trebaldi). Following the friendship duet between Alvaro and Don Carlos there was a pause. Warren seemed to be having difficulties beginning Don Carlos' aria. The great man gave a sigh. He was about to come to the 'O gioia' before the stretta. Suddenly he froze. Leonora's locket slipped from his hand, and he fell, according to the *Washington Post*, 'first with his chest, then with his head' to the ground. The fall was only too real. The audience took fright. At his side, the singer playing Alvaro cried out, 'Lennie, Lennie!' Stage hands ran onto the stage, where they saw blood dripping from his broken nose. Taking turns, the stage manager Osie Hawkins and the tenor Richard Tucker delivered mouth-to-mouth resuscitation to the lifeless man. Dr Adrian Zorgniotti, the Met's house doctor, could do nothing more than to confirm the baritone's death. A half hour passed in confusion. No one had dropped the curtain. At this point, Rudolf Bing, the director of the Met, came on stage and addressed the audience: 'This is one of the saddest moments in the history of this theatre. May I ask you all to stand. It is in memory of one of our greatest artists. I am sure you understand that the performance cannot continue.' It was only now that the colossus was carried from the stage. The critic at the *Washington Post* wrote that this evening at the theatre, which ended around the same time that the opera would have ended, had moved him more deeply than any opera could. In this way, Warren's total commitment—his readiness to sacrifice his own life—had had a final, decisive effect on the person who had criticized him so unjustly.

✳ ✳ ✳

The ageing singer stood upon the stage like a barely moveable piece of furniture. In all the trappings of her coloraturi. Once her voice had been considered unique. She so loved to sing. That was how she had got into opera—she had risen from being a singer in a provincial choir in Slovakia to become a global star of coloraturi: Rossini, Donizetti, Bellini, Verdi.

Now she herself had cancelled her engagement with the Bavarian State Opera. The intervals between her roles had become longer and longer. The critics, initially measured in their reactions, were becoming distinctly negative. A doctor told her that the vocal chords, which after all were only muscles, became weaker with age. She knew that herself, that the flow of air could no longer be pressed through this gate as precisely as it could in the past. She changed her doctor. The new one was more polite, but unable to offer her any comfort.

During a guest performance in an Eastern European country, where music wasn't treated quite so invidiously and competitively, the theatre's resident doctor sprayed her throat with a medication. Immediately she felt that she had regained the same command of the muscles of her vocal chords that she had had in the past. It was here that she dared to perform sotto voce the entire coloraturi of LINDA DI CHAMOUNIX in their original length. It turned out that the newly appointed artistic director of the Oslo opera house, on the lookout for young talent in the east, happened to be in the audience,. He fell in love with the great lady's voice, just as so many others had at the beginning of her career. He wanted to take her on. Earlier in the evening she had taken courage from the effects of the spray, but now, at the end of the gruelling performance, she found that her ambition did not extend to embarking on a new adventure of this kind.

❊ ❊ ❊

During the final rehearsals for his *Europeras 1 & 2* at the Frankfurt opera house in the autumn of 1987, John Cage was staying at the Hotel Frankfurter Hof. This meant that when he received the disturbing news that the opera house was on fire, he didn't have far to hurry to the scene. He took a tape recorder with him, and he had filled the pockets of his winter overcoat with various different kinds of special microphones. The city's fire brigade had several of its units ready for an assault on the stage house, the centre of the fire. In the meantime, a firestorm had already developed in this part of the opera house. It was simply too dangerous to send in the fire teams against it. They would have to let the fire burn.

It was only after the roof fell in, bringing a mass of building material down with it, that parts of the fire could be put out. Cage found that the acoustic power of a firestorm of this kind produced a sound he'd never heard before: an 'infernal hissing'. When he asked the fire chiefs about it, they explained that the sound was produced by the flames sucking the oxygen out of the surrounding air. A continuous noise could be heard on the tapes Cage used to record the sounds (he listened to them immediately afterwards, though the recording did not correspond to what he'd heard at the scene). He played it several times to other people present, including to members of the orchestra who were now appearing at the scene of the inferno. Cage had also recorded the high-pitched tone of the firemen's voices, caused by excitement and nervous strain, and the same phenomenon among several of the spectators.

In the days that followed, before the first performance of his two *Europeras*, which had now been postponed until 12 December, Cage acquired an audiotape from a sound technician at Hessischer Rundfunk containing recordings of the discharge and impact of shells fired from British 12-pounders, a type of heavy artillery. On the night before the premiere of his operas (the performance had been moved to

Frankfurt's main theatre), Cage packed his audiotapes and notes into a cardboard box. It contained the draft for his 'Suite for Cacophony and Orchestra', known as *Europera 2a*. Using the material he'd recorded at the opera house fire, Cage had tried to set to sounds the image of an air attack on Beirut. Along with the noises of the shell explosions (which he'd got from Hessischer Rundfunk) and the sounds of the fire at the opera house, Cage had included a passage from the last act of Bernd Alois Zimmermann's opera *The Soldiers* (containing no vocal music), and a page of sheet music that he'd sketched out in rough and which the members of the orchestra were to play on instruments of their own choosing according to a principle of random determination. This package, unmarked and unprofessionally tied together, was mistaken for rubbish by the hotel's chambermaid and thrown in the bin — lost sketch for sound and orchestra by John Cage.

✿ ✿ ✿

Shortly before his death, John Cage put together another package that has survived and whose content was recently made the subject of a performance by Heiner Goebbels in Baden-Baden. Following a long telephone conversation with his partner, who had caught the gruesome March flu that was raging along the east coast of the United States,

Cage wrote his 'Short Concerto for Cough (Deep in the Bronchials), Sniffling and Selected Notes by Bach, Schönberg and Myself'. The notes form an aleatory input, a kind of meal to which the soloists of the Ensemble Modern help themselves; their organized sound jostling with the breaks of something completely different, namely, the sounds made by the body when seized with the coughs and irritations of a cold. Cage claimed that nowhere else was there anything richer in variations than this forcing of the air from the stomach through the vocal chords and on into the head, accompanied by the bronchial tubes. It was, according to him, superior to the voices of opera singers. It had, he added, significantly more harmonics. Following a trans-Atlantic telephone call with his close friend Heinz-Klaus Metzger, he gave the piece the German title '*Rotz und Wasser*' — 'Snot and Water'.

❊ ❊ ❊

Stroke of luck. The spindly-limbed boy of about five ran down the jetty in great excitement, and with a cry of

— Yeah!

slipped as he ran over the topmost rung of the metal bathing ladder and tumbled, head flung back, over the side, missing by millimetres the hard metal edge that would have struck

the back of his head had he not reacted at just the right moment.

Thus the boy might easily have died, falling into the water and drowning after suffering a blow to his head. There were no experienced swimmers nearby who might have saved him, just well-meaning amateurs, and it is doubtful whether one of the elderly ladies watching what was happening from the shore would have done what was needed and told one of the waiters at the hotel, who might have been able to find an expert swimmer . . . All of this would have taken more time than the boy had left, had he not been lucky, a veering, hairpin luck, since the tiny reflex movement that saved him, a movement made as he fell, meant he just missed the rung by a slight tilt of his head.

Now the boy was swimming in the lake, shouting:

—I gotta do that again . . . !

He had, of course, neither realized what danger his young life had been in, nor that he had been the one who'd saved it—something in him, stronger than chance, that governed his movements on slippery surfaces.

✳ ✳ ✳

Walter Benjamin called one of the members of the Bauhaus he knew a 'CIRCUS DIRECTOR OF CHANCE'. The remark was intended to be encouraging. Training this UNRULY, CONSTANTLY SURPRISING, BREED OF REAL CONDITIONS THAT WE CALL CHANCE, which almost never conforms to any range of averages but which nevertheless orchestrates our individual fates and the circumstances of our lives, was, of course, difficult, he said. For him, this art was at its most consummate when chance events still occurred in their untamed or half-tamed condition while conforming to the law of form that holds sway beneath the circus tent. The tension between UNCON-TROLLABILITY and DISCIPLINE, between a chaotic basis (the ground on which the artistes could be smashed to pieces) and the trapeze above—this, says Benjamin, is the principle of art.

❊ ❊ ❊

A mother gazing at her infant in 1908. The curtains blew in the midday sun like sails filled with wind. The nursery windows looking out onto the garden stood wide open.

The child was asleep, with its arms resting on the covers so that it would not sweat. It pooped a few times, digesting its last meal. The young mother was waiting for her husband, who would be home for lunch punctually at one o'clock. The enzymes in his stomach and the sugar levels in his blood kept a clocklike regularity—everything else in life he treated with equanimity, except this. She had fed the child early so that everything would be ready when he arrived, and now she had time to wait.

The child's features reminded her of her favourite brother. But can one ever hope to find, in a creature who changes with every passing day, clear signs or similarities with other family members?

She would have been able to distinguish this child's features from all the other children in the world, no matter how upset or dirty its face might be, or how diffuse the light. But she wouldn't have been able to say which individual factors made up the general picture she had. The sleeping child's face was really nothing like the face that whined or laughed when it was awake.

In 36 years' time, this living being would be as old as she was now. That would be in 1944. The woman waiting for her husband didn't know that when air-raid sirens sounded in that far-off time, young women would be hurrying to the bunker beneath the Tiergarten's flak tower, a concrete structure surpassing every other stone monument, which was only definitively blown up three years after the end of the war.

❊ ❊ ❊

The cheeks, or rather chaps, reclining on a bed of grass. The forelegs relaxed. Dog asleep in the sun. The dog is called Leica. Named by his owner after the camera and not after the space heroine, Laika, the dog who fell victim to the impetuous attempt to conquer the cosmos.

The experts who sent Laika out into space couldn't bring her back. The real circumstances of her death were covered up by the space authorities. They never intended to have her return to earth. The Moscow street dog, who had been judged especially resistant to stress, died in agony of overheating before a fast-acting poison was able to kill her. In their hurry, the scientists who built the space capsule hadn't got around to fitting it with a reliable temperature regulator. This most noble of dogs could never be said to have 'lain' or 'stood' calmly in her cradle as it hurtled in orbit round the earth at 18,000 miles an hour.

As I said: the DOG LYING IN THE MORNING SUN has nothing in common with the dead space traveller—neither her fate, nor her name.

❊ ❊ ❊

Our dog had become cautious in her movements. Nothing remained of the clumsy, daredevil enthusiasm of her younger days. When faced by the step from the hallway to the kitchen, which at 30 centimetres was half the height that she was, she would run back and forth, hesitating before this chasm.

So it remained a mystery why (a few hours after we'd picked her up from the boarding kennels where she'd been staying while we were on holiday) she should have gone out onto the iron balcony on the second floor of the house, which overlooked the garden. It was somewhere she never went; but it was there—with the view over a tree whose leaves were moving gently in the summer wind, though with her eyes so ravaged by cataracts she can't have seen much—that she pushed herself between the balcony's narrow iron railings and, once she'd got about halfway through, lost her balance and fell.

Screams from a neighbour. The animal lay in the grass beneath the balcony and the tree, her teeth bared in shock.

Her legs were stretched out in front of her. Everyone who saw her said she lay there calmly. No, she didn't utter a single whimper or a single moan. She was either paralysed with terror or utterly calm. Someone fetched a cushion and a blanket from the winter-clothes cupboard. The neighbour and my wife gently wrapped her up in preparation for being taken away. While they were doing this, someone called a vet. Yes, they could come immediately.

In a moment of crisis, the hierarchy of comforters becomes clear. My wife urgently sought advice, despite the fact that what needed to be done was perfectly clear, and the neighbour supported her with practical suggestions. The neighbour held up one side of the cushion that the dog was lying on. My wife got hold of my daughter by mobile phone, who was having her hair cut at the hairdresser's. She cancelled the appointment. I'll call again tomorrow, she said. She got a taxi and rushed back.

At the vet's there was really nothing to decide. The vet suggested that we could still have the dog X-rayed at the clinic, but only for the sake of appearances, out of a kind of doctorly politeness. It would be better, of course, to have her put to sleep.

This was the 'final kiss of death', the only thing you could still do for the animal if you loved it. The dog's unbroken skin probably concealed the fact that, beneath it, its little body had been destroyed. The vet had given the dog, which lay there with its limbs stretched out rigidly in front of it, a shot of sedative in order to win time. Blood dripped out of its anus. Its hind legs did not react to any kind of stimulation. I'm assuming, said the vet, that her spine is broken. You have to make your decision. The dog's eyes gazed at us calmly. It's as if she's dreaming, said my daughter. She knew by our smell that we were there.

The dense emotional field which filled the room, and which the doctor was trying to steer towards a decision, remained immobile. The vet had filled the syringe, the 'kiss of death', and laid it next to the dog. A nod of consent from my wife and daughter indicated their permission.

The vet laid the cushion with the dog on it on a table in a room adjoining the surgery. You can say goodbye here, she said to the women. Over the next hour, the dog's body gradually grew cold. Arrangements were made for the animal's body to be cremated and delivered to our house the following week.

❊ ❊ ❊

One morning at four o'clock, the hour when the body is at its weakest, a young woman whose clinical condition had suddenly and drastically deteriorated found she was still able to see, albeit indirectly, the light of dawn. She saw it as a glimmer on the metal of the medical equipment that surrounded her. She could not see the window from her bed in the intensive care unit.

If, that is, there had in fact been any windows in the room, which was designed to keep the outside world at bay. She was still able to notice things. She registered that she had not expected to live to see the end of that terrible night.

City life began to flow through the hospital. The nurses and junior doctors hurried noisily about. And all at once she took hope, until at about seven o'clock in the morning when her circulation collapsed and, shortly after being given an extra shot of morphine, she died.

❊ ❊ ❊

Value of a child in wartime. A doctor from Saxony-Anhalt tells the following story: in December 1945, a wealthy farmer brought his daughter to me and asked that I help deliver her child. In the kitchen he set down a large ham. The examination revealed that the daughter was not due to give birth for a long time. The father adamantly insisted that I induce the birth. He thought there were drugs that could set off contractions.

Several days went by. The father returned with his daughter and again demanded with obdurate insistence that the birth be induced. There is no time to waste, he said. He offered a large sum, as if he were asking me to perform an abortion. No, he said, he didn't want an abortion. In any case, I replied, it wouldn't be possible at this late stage. No, what he wanted was an early birth, within the next few days, best of all right away. He added, in a confidential tone, that an early birth could be achieved by administering an oxytocic.

It turned out that the matter had to do with the end of
the war. In its final weeks, two of the farmer's army com-
rades had abused his hospitality and started a relationship
with his daughter. Of these two officers, one was penniless
while the other possessed a large fortune. The birth was taking too long to arrive. Another two weeks and it would be
clear, said the father, that the poor officer (the penniless one)
was the father. The day he had first come to the surgery with
his daughter, it could still have been the rich officer. I
returned him the ham untouched. Given the medicines

available in December 1945, no justification could be given for gratuitously inducing an early birth, whether for the good of the child or the mother, even though I could see that the child might have benefited from having a rich father. The father's struggle over the value of the child showed me that the war was over and the world had reverted to being a society based on exchange.

❊ ❊ ❊

Horror. During a shipwreck, a woman clung to her child as the water rose up to her waist while rescue teams could be heard working in the rooms next door. As the little whimpering creature struggled against her grip, the woman concentrated all her strength into holding on to it with her arms. At that moment, the ship listed sideways, and the woman, whose limbs seemed to have lost all sensation in the freezing water, slipped; she noticed that, though she was using every ounce of her strength not to reach for a handhold but to keep a firm grasp of the child, she now had no more strength to summon. As the bundle disappeared into the water, she tried to reach after it, feeling about in the swirling wash with deadened arms. It was while she was searching and feeling about that she was pulled out by the rescue team, wrapped in blankets and taken by stages to a specialist hospital,

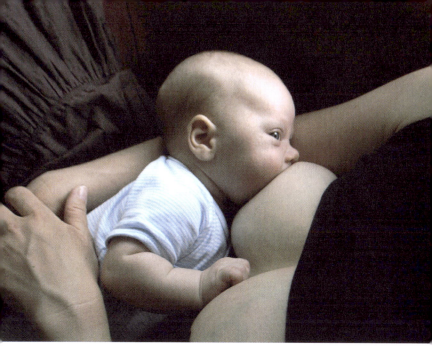

where she was treated for hypothermia. She sat on the adjustable hospital bed, her gaze fixed and her arms raised.

DOCTOR. How are we going to get her back to a normal life?

MOTHER SUPERIOR. We're keeping her under observation till tomorrow morning, in case she tries to harm herself. You should give her a sedative . . .

DOCTOR. I'd rather not, given the shock she's had . . .

MOTHER SUPERIOR. We don't have many precedents to go by, not even in this hospital . . .

DOCTOR. No.

MOTHER SUPERIOR. She has understood perfectly well what happened.

DOCTOR. Yes, but understanding doesn't mean that she's accepted it.

MOTHER SUPERIOR. No, she doesn't accept it. She wants to make it clear that she doesn't accept it.

DOCTOR. Even now?

MOTHER SUPERIOR. No, I don't think she accepts it at all.

DOCTOR. What can we do about such an attitude?

MOTHER SUPERIOR. I don't think we should do anything about such an attitude.

❊ ❊ ❊

The frog 'smells' the lilypads' bright blue flowers, though presumably he can't see them with his eyes. Frogs are short-sighted. The prince hidden inside them is not thought to be much of a colourist. Presumably the frog is more interested in having his hind leg stroked by a neighbouring frog than in the brilliant hues of the flowers. Things have been this way for a very long time. Turtles, by contrast, are very strongly attracted to colour. Their slow-moving, centuries-old eyes possess four colour receptors (while we human beings only have three). What would a painter paint if he could see the world like a turtle? Crocodiles, by contrast, inhabitants of the Nile, remain age-old and colour-blind.

❊ ❊ ❊

—You're talking about the catastrophe that wiped out 50 per cent of all the organisms on our planet, the Great Extinction?

—That's what we're working on. You know, we still don't completely understand why many species, like frogs, for example, managed to survive. With a sudden event of this kind, one would really expect only 'new formations' to develop in the 'niches' that had become available.

—But the frogs endured?

—Obviously. As if they'd been kissed by princesses.

—Given the kind of skin they have, their rather solemn and complex mating habits and the metamorphoses they go through in the course of their lives, they're excellent candidates for extinction. They're remarkably sensitive animals. Just look at their bellies!

—While all their neighbours died out, they were spared.

—Did living in ponds give them some kind of special protection?

—You mean more protection than deep-sea creatures or desert animals, all of whom died out? I don't think so.

—Something saved them. Perhaps their ugliness? The grace of God? Nature is unjust.

—Cruelly biased.

—Perhaps frogs have royal blood?

—That would be just as biased. Though it would explain the survival of the species. 'By the grace of God.'

—As a scientist, I can only explain it to you as a kind of miracle. The frogs survived the GREAT EXTINCTION, during which they were exposed for a hundred years to a sun darkened by dust and cloud masses.

—And could that have something to do with the morphology of frogs?

—You mean the fact that no one wants a frog for a lover?

—That could have been their lucky break—frogs were 'forgotten' by extinction.

❊ ❊ ❊

The moon, our constant companion. Shortly after the forma-
tion of the earth, after its iron core had already developed, a
large body must have collided with this conglomerate. This
event flung material out from the earth's mantle which then
formed into the moon.

The first rocks formed on the moon about 4.4 billion
years ago. Violent impacts between 4.3 to 3.9 billion years
ago hollowed out its giant maria. Lava forced itself upwards
from 500 kilometres beneath its surface. For the last 3 billion years, the moon has been tectonically dead, a 'prema-
ture birth'. The ebb and flow of powerful tides on earth are
caused by earthquakes on the moon, which extend deep
beneath its rocky surface. Near our companion's south pole,
where there were almost no lava flows, is the deepest of the
known maria of any moon in our planetary system. Many
craters on the south pole have never seen the light of the
sun.

2

In early August 2011, in one of Frankfurt's high-rise towers, sat one of the VETERAN TRAINERS OF CAPITAL. His eyes were fixed on his computer screen. At this height above the city, adjustable blinds over the windows muted the unimpeded effect of a glaring sun. Otherwise you wouldn't have been able to see much on the screen. The effect was to make the room look as if it were wearing sunglasses.

On this particular day, the experts were at a loss as to what to do. They watched the collapse of the stock market on a graph where a perpendicular line signalled the loss of four percentage points from the DAX in the space of less than four minutes. That was the equivalent of several billion dollars. In this darkened room up in the sky, the practitioner did not have a theory for what was happening. Does a lion tamer have a theory for lions? He knows his animals. The behaviour of these particular creatures, who were wreaking monstrous devastation on both sides of the Atlantic, was unfamiliar to the expert. Was it a new species? Or was it the crisis of 1929, merely in different guise? The legendary figure in his boardroom, normally an expert in restraining markets, would have liked to have been able to do something practical—crack nuts, peel an apple, pour himself a glass of mineral water—he longed for the comfort of any activity rather than having to wait staring at the screen.

✷ ✷ ✷

The wealth of the nation is invested in high-rise towers. One of these, made of glass and steel, is situated in the middle of Frankfurt am Main. Its caretakers, Herr and Frau Schmidtlein, were already guarding its entrance while its upper stories were still being built.

So what happens over the long weekends at this symbolic site of social wealth? No one lives there. Once, Herr and Frau Schmidtlein took a group of relatives from northern Hesse on a tour of the building's many floors. The security staff know the Schmidtleins and tolerate these kinds of visits.

How else could the building be used on the weekend? It may not be used as a dance hall. Nor as a theatre. When empty, it is placed under particularly heavy surveillance. Young people aren't allowed in. The building could be filled with weekend seminars. But the insurance won't allow it. Once a chamber music group, sponsored by Deutsche Bank, played in the corridors of the sixteenth floor. It turned out that the acoustics were pretty good. Sometimes on weekdays a woman comes from Giessen and runs a charcuterie stall on the second floor. The rest is offices. Very little human use value for so much architectural magnificence. 'Social wealth'.

❀ ❀ ❀

HIGH-RISE TOWER SEEMINGLY STAINED WITH RUST. The colour of the building's facade in New York is caused not by rust but by the reflection of a neighbouring skyscraper in its glass-and-steel facade. A sign of the finite nature of such tower blocks, should they ever be attacked by enemies. Below and to the right is a more traditional building. The windows of its top storey are surmounted by round and rectangular pediments. Stonemasons had to be brought from Europe to make them. Ornaments of this kind were not industrially produced. The university city at Princeton was built by skilled stoneworkers specially imported from Italy. Even they initially had to take special training courses, so they could give late medieval Gothic form to modern institutions of learning using the specialist tools of the early twentieth century. Why do buildings imitating much older ones appear more enduring than high-rise towers in New York, and since when have we seen them that way? 'New Unobjectivity'.

❊ ❊ ❊

The model of a city 'as on an alien planet'. The 'ruins of a city of the future' emerged from the sawn-off stump of a tree—the structure, caused by the tree being felled before

the saw passed cleanly through its middle, is tall and pointed, round and fibrous. That the loggers should have stopped their saw at precisely the moment that produced this structure is pure chance.

❊ ❊ ❊

A window overlooking railway tracks. Goods wagons are shunted here in summer and winter. The tracks they stand on connect them to all the other tracks of Europe. From here, you can send wagons westwards to Bordeaux and eastwards to Bucharest and beyond. A hundred and forty years ago, this network of tracks was still only sparsely developed. Over time, it became denser and was occasionally destroyed or broken up by borders. But the network of tracks prevailed. The railway siding at a concentration camp meant annihilation. For the people clinging to the sides of the last evacuation trains in 1945, railway lines could mean salvation.[1] Then there are childhood memories of wishing to become a conductor, a train driver or a stationmaster. Railways form a UNIQUE KIND OF CITY, the railway network.

❊ ❊ ❊

On his return from his trip to the United States, Heiner Müller (still energized by the days' rehearsals) expressed in the canteen of the Berliner Ensemble his thoughts on airports. You could say: 'Airports of all countries, unite!' That is, if all the runways and airport installations were lashed together into a kind of 'raft', they could, given that they are already so isolated from the cities they serve, rise up together into the air to form an imaginary space station, a SPACE CITY FOR PEOPLE IN A HURRY. Müller sketched out on a beer mat what he had in mind, explaining that current developments in global aviation technology already had the energies and potential to realize such a project. Indeed, it was far more likely that such an enterprise would arise by itself from the chaotic operations of global aviation. The problem was that combining all this potential (like combining the power of the proletariat) was unlikely to succeed in practice, and therefore the separation from the earth that a certain faction of humanity was clearly interested in was unlikely ever to happen. Müller could still feel the jetlag in his bones from his return flight from the western United States which had brought him via Dublin and Frankfurt to Tegel airport in Berlin.

❊ ❊ ❊

In the 1920s, Prussian minister of culture Carl Heinrich Becker and his wife bought a house in the small southern

German town of Kressbronn on Lake Constance. Kressbronn was a housing settlement artificially implanted in a rural area. After 1945, this country house became the Becker clan's retreat. It was here that his son Hellmut established both his family and his legal firm, which specialized in political and cultural matters. I worked for the firm during the advocacy stage of my legal clerkship. At that time, Kressbronn possessed a single cinema showing an irregular programme of films, and an elderly restaurant that dated from its days as a prospective spa town. The rest of the area was predominantly rural.

The part of the villa's ground-floor office that immediately surrounded the telephone possessed an urban character. Anything that was more than 3 metres away from this apparatus bore no relation to urban life whatsoever (apart perhaps from Hellmut Becker's books which lined the shelves in the dictating room; books are always urban). After a few weeks, I was 'pining for the city'. How swiftly the arrows of my desire, of my libido, flew ahead of me when some reason arose for a business trip to Frankfurt am Main! As I entered the city's suburbs, all my nerves would become agitated, as if by a stimulant.

Once I'd arrived in the city I found that I could sleep quite soundly, because so many other things (or at least, enough of them) were going on around me. I am not suited to living in the country. I AM PAROCHIALLY URBAN.

❊ ❊ ❊

Just what is a city? In his house in Starnberg, steps lead from the living room to the study where the scholar is sitting in front of his computer. His method of working at the computer is, however, merely a variation on writing with a pencil or pen on a sheet of paper. He still sketches out his thoughts not in a circle or a square but in a vertical rectangle, in other words, in the form of an A4 piece of paper. This lends his thinking a certain rhythm.

The project that Jürgen Habermas is currently working on has to do with the two so-called AXIAL AGES. These involve 'moments of progress in civilization that suddenly appear from nowhere'. For the CROOKED TIMBER OF HUMANITY, they always come unexpectedly and in the form of a dynamic that emerges in several different parts of the planet at the same time: between 5,000 and 3,000 BCE, and again at about 500 BCE. And in such a manner that it would seem as if a Creator had intervened or an evolutionary historical event had taken place, leading people to tolerate living in such proximity with one another. This project of modernity is called CITY.

Habermas, who can find no clear reason for the origin of this phenomenon, sees it as the beginning of a cosmopolitan society whose effects are being felt to this day, even if the projects of a new beginning associated with it have been lost or destroyed along the way. *That* something of this kind happened seems to him to be indisputable, but *what* brought it about is a matter of faith. Habermas (and in this he follows the sceptic Immanuel Kant) distrusts any 'faith in reason'. It could have been an error and it could have been a stroke of luck that brought forth such a CONSTELLA-TION AMONG HUMAN BEINGS (Confucius, Buddha, Heraclitus) in different places over a short period of time. But we need to think of it as a gift.

The sources and writings of religious faiths, which Habermas means respectfully to engage with, tell us very little about the two axial ages. The authorities of faith do not pride themselves on these two periods (the one exception being India). However, these 'world miracles of innovation' on the part of religions have left behind fragments and shards. It is a question of gathering these and surveying them. The scholar thinks of himself neither as a Cassandra nor as a prophet nor as a founder; he does not see himself as a land surveyor either but, rather, as a lawyer in disguise (just as Kant takes upon the roles of both presiding and assessor judge in a TRIBUNAL OF REASON). As such, he considers it valid and justified to think of human beings as citizens of the world.

✳ ✳ ✳

The tall archaeologist was sitting on a rock from where she could survey the entire excavation site of the former megacity of Uruk. The security detail was close by. She was not afraid of scorpions.

She dug into the sand of the site with her bare feet. She was waiting for her colleagues to return, who were pacing out the area of the invisible ancient city with measuring instruments, square metre by square metre. The instruments measured ground plans and stone structures hidden beneath the layers of earth. If you had five surveyors cover this trail for 10 hours every day for the next 25 years, then the area of the ruins would be fully measured out. Then you could draw up a complete map of Babylonian Uruk.

'One (whole) square mile is city /
One (whole) square mile is gardens /
One (whole) square mile is meadow /
One half square mile is the Temple of Ishtar.
The square miles and one half, that is Uruk, those are its dimensions!'[2]

While she waited (she was waiting in case one of her colleagues found something), the archaeologist's foot struck against a hard object. She picked up the piece of stone, which had been rubbed clean by the sand, and put it in her lap like a doll. It was a beautiful lion, a fragment with symbols inscribed on its base. She was able to read these symbols. She estimated this chance discovery to be about 4,000 years old. The inscription included a royal emblem.

'When his hand raised his sceptre /
The spirits of the dead began to tremble.'

The royal emblem on the base of the lion showed the archaeologist that the piece had come from very far away. The inscription was characteristic of a king who had never ruled in Uruk. Rather, this lion fragment originated from a place 200 kilometres away. The king of this distant realm had boasted of his conquests in the inscription on the lion. Bedouins must have discovered the object and brought it here. But why had they thrown it away? So that time and sand might conquer it? The ruler the stone lion had belonged to had no connection with Uruk. The robbers had travelled great distances. Their greed moved like the wind. Their indifference, however, also moved like the wind, when they found something better. Evidently the robbers had found something better on the site of Uruk, something that was clearly heavy, and which they guessed they could more easily sell for silver to the British or some other interested party than the stone fragment that the archaeologist found so marvellous. So they had got rid of the fragment.

'But the gods smell the scent /
The gods smell the sweet scent /
The gods congregated as quickly as flies /
Upon him who had given sacrifice.'

❊ ❊ ❊

One of the fellows at the Institute for Advanced Study in Berlin gave a report on the work of Hungarian scholar Julian Jaynes. Jaynes made the claim that the early founders of the cities of Mesopotamia, above all Uruk (and later also the heroes of the *Iliad*, such as Achilles, Ajax or Odysseus, whose 'heart roared within his chest'), possessed the same kind of physiological brain that we do today but used it differently, namely, bicamerally. The right half of the brain, which understands language but which is not responsible for speech, was the domain of the voices of the gods, while the left hemisphere served the understanding of everyday life.

According to him, it was this that determined the fact that it was ALL AT ONCE, and not GRADUALLY BY THE AMALGAMATION OF VILLAGES AND HAMLETS, that the first cities, that is, the FIRST GREAT CIVILIZATION came into being. This, claimed the fellow, took place like an explosion.

The necessary preconditions for this 'single authentic revolution by the human race' (quickly overwhelmed by counter-revolutions and only briefly re-emerging in sudden spasms) are drugs, religion and a regular supply of foodstuffs from plantations and greenhouses as well as cooperation. The voices of the gods in people's heads and the tolling of the bells of the ziggurat, that is, the voices of the dead kings, create an inner world across the narrowest space imaginable. This is the CITY AS POLITY. Earlier, human beings living at such close quarters would have beaten one another to death. THE CITY EVOLVED TOLERANCE.

❊ ❊ ❊

In a chest, excitedly unpacked in the United States by Theodor W. Adorno and his companion Löwenthal in the hope that it might contain the legendary ARCADES PRO-JECT, a piece of paper was discovered with a note that, since it appears in his handwriting, has long been attributed to Walter Benjamin. The paper contained a record of a conversation between Benjamin and Alfred Sohn-Rethel. The title of the text is as follows:

The city's capacity for abstraction. Geneva as example.

It notes that Calvin established a theocracy in the city of Geneva. Calvin had one of his friends, a doctor and a theologian, burnt at the stake as a result of theoretical religious differences. In spiritual matters, the settling of accounts is strict. Geneva, however, was also one of the origins of the WESTERN IDEA OF FREEDOM (which spread through the Netherlands to Scotland, and was then brought

by the pilgrim fathers to Boston). DECREASE IN TOL-
ERANCE, INCREASE IN FREEDOM.

A businessman from Geneva by the name of Henry
Dunant, continues Sohn-Rethel in his text, a speculator,
makes his way to the headquarters of Emperor Napoleon
III in Castiglione. He requests an audience. He would like
to acquire licences to operate mills in in Algeria. This happens on the evening before the battle of Solferino. The
emperor has no time to grant him an audience. Later, the
businessman from Geneva is shocked at the sight of the
wounded on the battlefield. Henry Dunant writes a book.
The appeal it launches leads to the founding of the Red
Cross. Shortly afterwards, this man's private business deal-
ings result in a RUINOUS BANKRUPTCY. The Red
Cross, however, transforms the general impulse towards
BENEVOLENCE, which has developed as a 'weak power'
in human evolution, into a radical abstraction: THE RED
CROSS OFFERS HELP IN ADVERSITY WHILE
REMAINING NEUTRAL. The point is to reach the
wounded, the victims. Nothing, not human sympathies, not
even moral indignation with war and those who wage it,
should come in the way of helping the victims. This was
why, during the Abyssinian War in which the Italian army
used poison gas, a senior consultant of the Red Cross
refused to hand over the medical records of his field hospital

to the League of Nations. The GENEVA ABSTRACTION (which, though it appears to disregard empathy, is in fact founded upon an enduring empathy, an 'urban tolerance') is part of the 'idea of the West'. It is, according to Sohn-Rethel's note, a reminder of the phrase: 'First human beings do something, then they understand what they are doing, and in this way philosophy comes into being.'

❊ ❊ ❊

Peter Schäfer, the Judaist from Princeton, was asked how the four rivers of the Babylonian Talmud, which surround paradise, should be interpreted, given that of the four rivers we know only the rivers Euphrates and Tigris. Schäfer identifies paradise with the founding of the early megacities. It was only here that lions and gazelles lay down together, peacefully, as it were, in a manner that reflects the evidently sudden (and temporary) harmoniousness among the people of the time. This paradise, says the Talmud, has been lost.

❊ ❊ ❊

While being interviewed about his study of the megacities of our world, Richard Sennett was asked by a reporter from the *Financial Times* whether there was any contemporary city that was the reason behind his vehement defence of the

urban principle. The suburbs of Chicago, where he came
from, could hardly, she suggested, have been the basis for
this affinity. Sennett hesitated a long time before answering.
In Lagos, he had seen slums where desperately poor people
had furnished their homes in a manner that astounded the
visiting planners and researchers. But then he decided he
would answer the question in the negative. No, there was
no city he knew of that was the reason for his attitude
towards 'urban public life'. The city that we carry around
inside ourselves, he said, is invisible. But when you see a

city destroyed by bombs, one which you do not know and means nothing to you, and you nevertheless feel sad, then you can see from this reaction that we carry around inside ourselves just such an invisible city. You see the city only when it has been lost.

3

COLUMNS THAT ONCE SUPPORTED AN UPPER STOREY HANG IN THE AIR LIKE UPROOTED TREES. On 26 April 2012, Gerhard Richter photographed this makeshift building site in Beirut. He was in the city for an exhibition of his work at the BEIRUT ART CENTER. He took a taxi to tour the city.

The building is separated from the city around it by a metal fence which rises the entire height of its facade. It is similar to the fences that protect audiences from wild animals at the circus. The ruins are awaiting their reconstruction. The holes in the masonry look like shell holes.

Since the supporting columns no longer reach the ground, the basement must first grow up to meet them. A stage in the renovation of the building. The traffic lights are showing red. In its ruined state, the building possesses Levantine, Byzantine and European features.

❊ ❊ ❊

During the Lebanese civil war, there stood near the edge of the centre of Beirut, on the southern side of the city, still within the zone of destruction wrought by the air attacks, the ELDORADO cinema, a cinema *in extremis*. It had been razed to its foundations. The couple who'd run the cinema for decades had cleared away the rubble and erected a tent on the level concrete surface where it once stood. Beneath this tent they set up the projectors they had saved. In front of these they set out several rows of chairs (makeshift chairs taken from a coffee house) and in front of these a screen. During screenings, the film's soundtrack would mix with the noise of battle as it approached and receded. The spectators were slightly safer beneath the tent than they would have been inside a solid building, since ruined buildings were seldom attacked a second time, and there was no danger of getting buried by falling masonry in the 'cinema hall'.

The couple, who had faithfully kept the cinema going, carried on their struggle with hopelessly meagre resources. Nevertheless, the seats beneath the tent were always full.

There was no box office, any more than there was any specific entrance; instead, entrance fees were gathered by passing a collection plate among the audience. The cinema would show *Pirates of the Caribbean* one evening, two Indian melodramas the next and then *The Promise* (by Chen Kaige). The ELDORADO was supposed to be an art-house cinema. Its two owners, however, had to use whatever films they were able to get hold of, irrespective of whether they conformed to any kind of programme. People found this emergency cinema comforting. They would sit (given that, unlike the rich, they didn't have the means to flee the city) very convivially together in the middle of the danger. It didn't matter what the programme was showing, as long as the projectors were running. These antiquated models had a crank that could be used to keep them going by hand in the event of a power cut.

❊ ❊ ❊

While renovating a series of basement floors in Beirut that extended for eight levels below ground (the building above had been destroyed in the civil war that had gripped the city), the French-Romanian engineer Olteanu discovered a buried hoard of treasure. It consisted of a intact cellar stocked with supplies dating to Phoenician times that had apparently been stored here in reaction to an assault upon the city, which at the time was not yet called Beirut, by ship-borne SEA PEOPLES over 3,000 years ago. Spices, of a variety unknown today, which had petrified over the centuries, were found stored in chests and barrels. Silver and gold coins. Purple-dyed robes that for some inexplicable reason had survived, as well as cloths (frayed, threadbare and faded, but still recognizable in their original condition, and, as long as you didn't touch them, more or less intact). These cloths had been dyed using a different kind of sea creature to the murex snail, producing a 'ghostly blue' more thrilling to the eye than any purple. The treasures, above all, the seeds (had Monsanto been able to patent them, they would have represented billions of dollars on the stock market), were archaeologically recorded but then (after tiny samples had been taken) left in the chamber where they were found, which, by virtue of the particular chemistry of the salts in the ground beneath Beirut, had evidently helped preserve this discovery.

Plans for constructing a new building on top of this treasure trove were postponed and the resulting losses written off. The Societé anonyme de Beyrouth, a public limited company, listed enormous gains on the Zurich stock exchange because it had acquired the hoard from the construction company in charge of renovating the basement floors.

✣ ✣ ✣

Levels of history. When part of the Roman province of Syria, Mount Lebanon and the Anti-Lebanon, so poetically described in the Song of Songs, possessed no distinguishing features. There was nothing that specifically identified them as a province in themselves. It was to these mountains that members of the Druze religious community fled in 1021. They were knights and feudal landowners who had been persecuted and driven from their original titles and estates. They believed the Fatimid Caliph al-Hakim to be the incarnation of God.

Their enemies, who had murdered this Caliph, vehemently disputed this claim. Like Shiism, the Druze religion emerged from mourning around a fatal loss. The mourning is linked to the certainty that an OVERTURNING OF ALL CONDITIONS will come at the end of the world. The regions occupied by the Druze were not fully contiguous. The spaces between them were settled by Syrian Christians and Syrian Jews. Unlike the Orthodox Christians or the Aramaics, they spoke not Greek but Arabic and, in the nineteenth century, it was from their descendants that teachers emerged whose learning would restore the 'pure Arab language'.

✣ ✣ ✣

In 1800, 8,000 people were living in Beirut. In 1860, there were 60,000. However, in the years up until 1860, a third of the population emigrated from Mount Lebanon and Beirut to such places as Latin America and the United States. From 1840 onwards, there was civil war. The provincial governors of the Ottoman Empire did little to protect the population and were unable to keep the warring parties apart. European powers gave guarantees and sent ships. Landing forces intervened.

The French Empire under Napoleon III supported the Christian Maronites, who were soon speaking French. In the following decades, the British Near East Administration would favour the Druze. Great economic hopes were placed upon the Near East. Stock markets were poised.

❊ ❊ ❊

In the empire of Napoleon III, the unofficial national anthem played on all ceremonial occasions from 1860 onwards was the song 'Partant pour la Syrie' ('Departing for Syria'). It was sung to evoke the spirit of Bonaparte's Egyptian campaign and his advance on Acre, in much the same way that, after 1807, Egyptian props and pyramids infiltrated stage designs for Mozart's *Magic Flute*.

Partant pour la Syrie,	On leaving for Syria
Le jeune et beau Dunois	The handsome young Dunois
Venait prier Marie	Offered prayers to the Virgin
De bénir ses exploits:	To bless his exploits:
Faites, reine immortelle,	Vouchsafe, Immortal Queen,
Lui-dit en partant,	He said as he took his leave,
Que j'aime la plus belle	That I should love the fairest
of women	
Et sois le plus vaillant.	And be the bravest of men.

In an age of world fairs and industry, a need for theatre arose — the romantic allusion to the age of the Crusades. 'He

carved in stone his oath of honour.' The years from 1860 to 1870 were marked in the West by a collective longing to find in the Levant, the land of the rising sun, restitution for all the privations of a disappointing series of revolutions and an enervating era of capitalism. 'A treasure lies hidden in the mountains of Lebanon.'

'This cherished union, which alone brings happiness.' This was 'love without recompense' and 'courage without reason', which could only be found and realized in the Orient. France's illusionists were so skilled that they knew that the gates into a historical parallel universe, the world as crystal ball, lay where Bonaparte was on the point of achieving his aim of reaching India, but failed to get as far as Acre. Between the mountains and the sea, by the cedars of Lebanon, very few of which still existed, lay the entrance to paradise, which, anti-clerical France would claim, men had mistakenly expected to find in Jerusalem.

On lui doit la Victoire.	They owed him victory.
Vraiment, dit le seigneur;	Truly, said the lord,
Puisque tu fais ma gloire	Since you have given me glory
Je ferai ton bonheur.	I shall make your happiness.
De ma fille Isabelle,	Take thou this day the hand
Sois l'Epoux à l'instant,	Of my daughter Isabelle,

| Car elle est la plus belle, | For she is the fairest of women |
| Et toi le plus vaillant. | And you the bravest of men. |

❊ ❊ ❊

Episode of the German empire in Jerusalem. In 1917 there arrived in Jerusalem, as if the edicts of twelfth-century caesars were still reverberating in the twentieth—something that is neither physically possible nor realistically feasible — 17 luminaries of German medical science. With its 17 reserve field hospitals, the city's medical facilities had the capacity to treat more patients than there were wounded men, whether they were Turks, injured Germans or natives. Junior doctors and senior nurses from noble families had arrived along with the leading physicians (having overcome the numerous inconveniences of the Baghdad railway which at the time existed largely only on paper, including having to change trains at the natural barrier of the Anatolian mountains). All this was under the command of Colonel General von Falkenhayn, appointed chief of the general staff in November 1914 but later demoted, frustrated, the victor over the Romanians, a second-rate adversary, hungry for results, irascible and eager to wrest the Suez Canal from the British. The German plan to turn Jerusalem into a sanatorium for every disorder still seemed feasible in the autumn of 1917, when the sense that they were winning the war still lingered and the general outlook did not appear altogether hopeless, and it was not because the British attempted to surround the Germans in what would later become the Gaza Strip that the plan failed but, rather, because the supply route for the German-Turkish army collapsed.

They should have relied on the help of the Lebanese merchants, the descendants of the Phoenicians. These merchants from Beirut could have supplied any army. In the regional German headquarters, however, racist and national prejudices stood in the way of any collaboration. The Maronites, skilled in trade, had 'Oriental', olive-skinned faces. They spoke French, which made them suspicious. The Turkish authorities participated in the repressive measures. When the German-Turkish army attempted to seize all foodstuffs for itself, a catastrophic famine broke out in the Lebanese mountains. More than 100,000 people died. Before the German army had even left Jerusalem, both the stock market in Alexandria and the cities of the Levant had lost any faith in their victory.

Several of the German medical experts, surrounded by people with doctoral degrees in their respective fields of study, each of them a brilliant surgeon, who represented the face of 'salvation' in Jerusalem, could not understand why they—the Crusaders, as it were, of the twentieth century—

should have to leave the city with such ignominious haste. Not all of them managed to get back to their universities by way of Constantinople and the Black Sea. During the brief period that the field hospitals were operating in the capital of Christianity, several medical innovations had been developed. Most of the documents were lost on the flight home.

✻ ✻ ✻

For a total of 11 mornings in the year 1898, Karl May worked on a new adventure novel that was to be set in the land of the Druze, a land that, at that time, he had never visited. The Druze, he noted, are powerful feudal lords, and they are in the minority next to the Maronite Christians and the Muslim immigrants from Palestine and Syria, who are moving into the valleys of the Chouf Mountains and threatening the Druze as they sheltered in their mountain strongholds. However, May had read or misunderstood somewhere that the Druze also rule over subterranean realms.

In these subterranean realms, the Druze own workshops where metalsmiths kidnapped from the world above are forced to labour for them. The workshops are reached through a cave entrance which initially leads into a chamber full of stalagmites. It is here that Kara Ben Nemsi, as he's called in May's outline, boards a boat and travels along dangerous subterranean streams and lakes, ever deeper into the mountain. There he frees not only the forced labourers but also a pack of children who are toiling away by torch-light. After a return journey fraught with adventure, he re-emerges to be met by his British friend, who takes him under his wing and brings him to the coast, all the while rebuking him for his 'irresponsible recklessness'. The children are delivered to a monastery, from where they are brought to safety in Cyprus.

May did not go on to develop this outline. But until he visited Beirut in 1899, the CHOUF MOUNTAINS

continued to capture his imagination, not least the word itself, which he'd discovered in geography books and dictionaries. Later when he did visit Lebanon, May learnt that there was indeed a mountain range of this name in the heartlands of the Druze but that none of the features that he had mentioned in his outline were to be found there. There were, however, ravines and cedars. May even found a subterranean lake during an excursion to the foothills of Mount Lebanon, where you could have yourself rowed across a flooded cavern. But the cave did not lie in the Chouf Mountains.

✳ ✳ ✳

From 1929 to 1931, the young officer Charles de Gaulle served as a training instructor in Beirut. The military installations in the mandate territory were low, white structures built with narrow, oblong windows. Similar in style to the windows of French light armoured cars while their interior furnishings recalled the elegant interiors of France's submersibles. Expressive will of the engineers and designers of modernity.

After finishing military school in St Cyr, a French officer with any ambition had to do everything he could to avoid being buried in the torpor of one of his country's own provinces. He had to look for an overseas command, for a posting in a place where innovation and adventure were possible, in order to manage from there the leap to the Ministry of Defence in Paris. Once he did that, all positions were open to him. In the nineteenth century, sought-after posts of this kind could be found 'on probation' in Algeria; after 1918, they could still be found in Lebanon.

Airstrips had been newly built by the mandate government. The national emblem of this 'land without self-government' was the French flag with a green cedar on a white field. The barracks and officers' quarters that the occupying power had recently built formed their own enclosure, a kind of fortress that was designed by military engineers who had been influenced by the construction methods of the Maginot Line. The difference was that in the mandate all the parameters of innovation could be more systematically implemented. Among these were a new form of war, as if the First World War, the JUST WAR, had (in the view of the experts) in reality been a defeat, which had to be learnt from in preparation for the impending decisive conflict of the twentieth century. Thus it was that, for these two crucial years, de Gaulle remained far removed from the administrative and planning centre that was Paris. Nevertheless, he found himself in a hotbed of innovation, where the ideas for a future war were being developed. There was, however, no opportunity of putting into practice his new concept of a combined armoured corps before 1940. One result of training Lebanon's military cadres, whom de Gaulle indoctrinated with his CONSERVATIVE MODERNITY, was that in November 1943 the Lebanese government unilaterally abolished the French mandate and, following the brief arrest of its members, demanded its independence.

❊ ❊ ❊

A group of German travellers from Opladen, tourists among borderlands. They were members of a society calling itself the KNIGHTS TEMPLAR. In 2012, after crossing the Mediterranean by ship, they took several buses from the city of Sidon to the Syrian-Lebanese border. It was there

they opened the sea containers that had travelled with them, unpacking weapons and chain mail, faithful reproductions of original historical models, and dressed themselves up as crusader knights. Looking like a group of hikers, only equipped for another age and seeming to come from another world, they marched like holidaymakers along the border between the two countries, following paths that they took to be the remains of an eleventh century main road. Behind themselves they pulled carts.

Soon they were spotted by the warlords who were controlling that particular area and defending it against Assad's armed forces. Towards evening, as the group of hikers was approaching a hamlet, they were surrounded by armed men and arrested. What use were the longswords they'd brought with them, and all the historical knowledge they had? The modern potentates kept the German citizens in a vaulted cellar for several weeks, freeing them only after the German consul general in Beirut had delivered their ransom. The kidnappers burnt their victims' fancy dress, so as to leave no trace of their crime nor of the whereabouts of the ransom money.

4

Lothar Müller writes that the concept of the present and a consciousness of contemporary history in terms of the topicality of daily newspapers have existed since about 1800. It is the urban news network, represented by the rhythm of morning, afternoon and evening papers in Europe's capital cities, that constitutes the matrix of topicality in people's minds, the changing flow of relevant facts. The element of this news world is surprise. A prohibition on repetition holds sway. News must be fresh. Like the dome of lights over a great city, the STATE OF THE NEWS forms an aura in which a general notion of what matters in the world coalesces.

It is out of such NEWS VALUES, and not out of the facts themselves, that the daily image of the reality of our world is put together. The products of poetry form an antithesis to this daily fluctuation. In painted images, and in the narratives of short stories and novels, time outside stands still.

✳ ✳ ✳

The journalists attending were uneasy. Two elderly criminals, brothers, one of whom had murdered a policeman (and who had been sentenced to life imprisonment and let out after serving 19 years), had, following a short argument, shot dead two policemen who were pursuing them and severely wounded one of their female colleagues. This, it was claimed, had happened after a high-speed chase and an earlier exchange of fire. Apparently the situation had turned against the pursuing policemen, who were no match for the experienced criminals and who recognized the danger they posed only too late. After one of the officers, who was significantly younger than the criminals, was left lying on the ground with gunshot wounds, the older of the two criminal brothers is said to have shot him a point blank range with an automatic pistol, putting several bullets into his neck, head and abdomen; of these shots, three were fatal.

The police spokesman, who was acting under orders, did not want to expressly mention the word 'execution'. He was still talking about the 'suspects', although, as one of the journalists pointed out to him, the criminals had been arrested at the scene of the crime, and one had a previous conviction for murdering a policeman. Yes, there was evidence, replied the spokesman, and the murder weapons were being tested for a DNA match. Although the investigators had not omitted anything from their presentation, neither had they emphasized the brutal way in which the killers had committed their crime.

The journalists, forced to compete with national papers, needed a juicy title for the five weekday editions between Christmas and the New Year, something like 'Properly Put

To Death'. However, the prosecutor in charge of the case and the head of the murder squad both agreed that, in order not to inflame 'a situation that is terrible enough as it is', it would be in the interest of the investigation and the trial to follow to say as little as possible. This, though, was precisely what the journalists needed from the spokesman—an officially sanctioned expletive. You can develop what I say in your own words, replied the spokesman, you just have to give the facts. No, the opinion makers wanted an official police definition of the extraordinary events which could be used in the headlines to their articles.

❊ ❊ ❊

They had been life-long friends, insofar as, when it comes down to it, careerists can ever be friends, and later they liked seeing each other for purposes of mutual benefit, and neither ever entirely lost sight of the other.

They were young. The alarm clock went off (in the form of the telephone at the paper's main news desk) at 10.20 p.m. Their chartered helicopter took off at about 11 p.m. It quickly brought them to the Belgian coast, to a port. A Channel ferry had sunk. People had drowned.

Taking down the horror in note form, making sentences out of it; they divided up the night between themselves. They didn't try to go everywhere—you have to *judge* the

situation. One of them, Till, went to the hospitals; the other, Gert, to the rescue divers — letting someone else get the chance of a big news scoop takes a lot of trust. They trusted each other . . . There's so much you can get wrong: the dead stored in a hall belonging to the Belgian army, the floor awash with seawater as fishermen wheel in the bodies, bright lights (hurriedly set up) — all these things had to be photographed, but you could not spend too much time on them. You can't expect to find any stories here, the fishermen don't want to talk, they're anxious to disappear because as long as they're here they aren't earning anything, no catch, just dead bodies—and even if one of them could be revived, the terrible thing is that he would earn the man who saved him nothing more than thanks. He is not worth what a hundredweight of fish would be worth.

The two friends flew several times over the stricken, listing ship in their chartered helicopter. There was little enough to see: the blinding glare of another helicopter's searchlight reflected on the side of the ferry, teams of divers being brought in—all this had to be photographed, even though it wouldn't produce any pictures.

They talked to the fishermen. The fishermen replied: 'They need to announce a recovery fee for dead bodies and a special prize for saving people who are still alive, a prize awarded by the governor. If they did, we'd find a lot of things of value in the waves right after accidents of this kind. We first went there out of curiosity. If only we'd resisted it! We have our doubts whether—in a world that's overpopulated, where the seas are overfished—people making cheap ferry crossings from France to England have any significant value at all. On the other hand, if there were prizes available it would at least be worth our while to wait outside the harbour for an accident to happen, since the prize we'd collect for each person we saved would pay for our trouble.' A form of beachcombing.

❉ ❉ ❉

On a Miami Beach houseboat, FBI investigators confiscated a total of 51 objects that were indirectly related to 27-year-old Andrew Cunanan, the murderer of Gianni Versace.

—At first it was claimed that Cunanan had been infected with AIDS and was taking exemplary revenge on his homosexual lovers.

—Or that he harboured a grievance.

—Or that the victims may have been connected to one another in some way. This is what people looking for some kind of logic characteristically hope to find.

—But it was none of these things. It seems he just killed anyone he had happened to run into.

❅ ❅ ❅

Art photography arising from a misunderstanding. After answering the telephone while his relative was away, the cousin of a highly esteemed photojournalist in Paris mistakenly received an assignment from *Le Monde* to photograph the imminent intervention by French helicopters and parachutists in Mali. Embedded with the troops and in online contact with his employer, he arrived in Timbuktu the same week. He was, however, a fine-art photographer, not a reporter. At first no one noticed—he concentrated on what was going on around him, threw himself into the work without really understanding what he was doing, and generally let himself be guided and prompted by what there was to photograph, recording the troops as they prepared for their mission. The action unfolded inside a tent. Weapons and munitions were stored here that the soldiers were carefully arranging for use. All this produced pictures that were suitable for publishing in a newspaper. There were scarcely any possibilities for variation.

But then, in Timbuktu, the artistic motifs started to accumulate. The artist was interested in a large ant which was crawling across the yard towards the desert. He photographed

several clumps of young palms which were struggling for life against the sand. One beautiful picture was of the foaming waters beneath a small waterfall. The captivating red of the horizon at evening, with the silhouette of a building on the right. The chief editor and the news team at *Le Monde* were puzzled by the pictures that were coming in. But then they found they actually liked the artist's photographs. Once a caption had been added, the pictures' lack of thematic clarity helped bring to life its recorded detail of reality. One of the photographs showed a detail of a marble tile covered in scratches, as well as cracks visible in the stone. In the room that the Islamists had burnt, this tile looked like a fragment from the ancient past. It turned out that French chasseurs, seconded from the expeditionary force that was occupying Egypt, had dined and spent the night there in 1799. The photographer sent the photograph with a text message explaining this. The editor-in-chief said that, unlike all the other photographs that had appeared in the press the same day, this one significantly broadened the definition of current affairs interest. In the meantime, the famous photojournalist had turned up, the cousin whom the artist had been mistaken for. They could have sent him out, since the French president was about to visit Timbuktu. But the editor of *Le Monde* found he liked the amateur photographs taken by the man who had been sent out by mistake. He left him in the job.

❊ ❊ ❊

For many centuries, thousands of monks in monasteries between Ireland and Byzantium, dotted like islands across the barbaric land, were writing out the holy texts. Their zeal and their great efforts produced mistakes. The result was that the texts imperceptibly expanded. One learned monk in Salamanca was delighted to find a text by Ovid on the back of a copy of the apocryphal LOGION OF ST JOHN. The copyist on the island of Reichenau could not resist including this interpolation. In this way, a text was expanded in a distinctly 'unholy' manner.

A transcription of texts (just as if evolution had been tinkering with their DNA texts) doesn't only create lines to new, future texts. It can also be reconstructed in the direction of paradise. The way there leads through indeterminacies. 'Nearer, my God, to Thee' was the music played by the orchestra on board the Titanic as the ship went down. But it is also the working instructions to copyists of all countries, who are driven from the omphalos of experience into the parallel world (heterotopia), the pre-world (history) and the future world (the world of our children, who are so attached to life). For copyists, all images are NOW-TIME.

❉ ❉ ❉

The determined tyranny of my mother's sharp eyes. Not a single stain on one's clothes escaped them. They would immediately detect a weakness in their opponent while her mouth, out of politeness, stayed silent. When she cried, my mother's gaze would lose its sharpness. Nor were her moods and intuitions ever as perceptive as her eyes.

✻ ✻ ✻

It was while out taking his exercise, crunching over the sand and gravel of Helgoland's windswept coast, that Werner Heisenberg had his legendary idea—the INDETERMINACY PRINCIPLE.

Since then, physics has come to regard it as a law of nature. You can either determine the momentum of an elementary particle or its position. This is not the effect of some deficiency in our measuring instruments or the limited scope of our present state of knowledge, but a basic characteristic of nature. It unfolds two parallel worlds. Between them, 'noise' prevails; one cannot exist without the other. Together they are real.

The indeterminacy principle also applies to human relations, for entirely different reasons than it does to physics. In this respect, keeping a lens out of focus—that is, giving it a focus that is *indeterminate*—is not a technical device but a response to a manifold reality. Certain reproductions are, so to speak, indeterminate by nature. What is more, authentic images always refer to something that lies outside the frame. Thus fimmakers such as Ernst Lubitsch, Fritz Lang, Hans Richter or Sergei Eisenstein have developed their art to such a degree that the most important impressions the viewer takes away from them are of a series of events outside the film.

Montage also produces 'invisible images'. If the film is well made enough, they will necessarily arise in the viewer's mind. Two incongruous scenes provoke a 'third image', the epiphany. Only those films that achieve this effect become part of film history. The musical equivalent to this filmic succession of 'unseen images' is harmonics. From Monteverdi to Cage, they form the true choruses.

John Cage's composition, which is being performed at the Church of St Buchardi in Halberstadt, leaves a whole year between its notes to allow for the piece to incorporate 'natural sounds'. These could be the footsteps and the hushed voices of visitors to the church. The sheep kept on the green outside the church could also contribute chance sounds to these intervals of tonality.

❉ ❉ ❉

Is it possible to inhabit a 'state of indeterminacy'? At a debate on the differences between architecture and art held at Lady Foster's house in S-chanf in the Engadine, a young artist asked this question so dogmatically that the pragmatic David Chipperfield immediately tried to contradict him. Niklas Luhmann writes that happy couples actually live in a kind of LEARNT INDETERMINACY. Without this indeterminacy, their 'characters', that is to say, their specificities (the fact that they could not merge and would have to die bolted or riveted together), could not come to any kind of agreement when they needed to.

To what degree do we *inhabit* our relations, Chipperfield asked his audience. There is, he claimed, an architecture of coexistence: consideration for others. Soothing convention.

Honourableness. Just as there is an ARCHITECTURE OF REASON, added his neighbour. Comments followed in quick succession. No one present wanted to grant natural laws the sole privilege of being indeterminate. Thomas Demand, who had earlier described the precision of architecture and the subjectivity of art as being opposed to each other, interjected that people live indeterminately by nature. If they paid no heed to indeterminacy, people would hurt one another.

Bazon Brock added that, since we are on the subject, even concepts are only able to relate to each other with a certain degree of indeterminacy.

❊ ❊ ❊

László Moholy-Nagy was asked whether a photograph reproduces a piece of reality. He denied the claim. He replied that a photograph is constituted by the fact that it concentrates on an actual moment and records it, becoming a textual addition existing outside the world. He knew, the Bauhaus man continued, series and networks of such photographs, which relate to reality or current events like a mirror (including to the gaps in that reality, to a silence or to a nothingness), but which, when cut off from the rapidly receding stratification of time, would form themselves into their own republic, one that would superimpose itself (like an El Niño mudslide) onto the original impression that

caused the photograph, which itself would have soon disappeared from the participants' memory, had they ever had the impression to begin with.

What this means, said Moholy-Nagy (who thought that photography had far better things to do than represent reality), is that all camera images produced by human beings tell a parallel history—an ideal landscape. Photographs, he added, are an ideal reservoir for insights when formulating observations of a second order, in other words, they are the triggers and detonating caps for art.

❊ ❊ ❊

I take a photo. A moment is recorded in it. The skin of the image consists of a thin layer that could almost be called 'non-material'. What the image records, the exposure, is not something material like paint applied to canvas or ink dabbed on a piece of paper. In digital photos, this 'technical spirituality' is even more intense.

At the same time, one cannot speak of a 'crystallized moment'. The instant of time that the photo wins from the intractable flow of reality is shorter than the blinking of an eye (the German word for 'moment', *Augenblick*, literally means the 'glancing of an eye'), it is shorter even than the eye's own capacity to distinguish the objects it sees. A photo should be called a 'detail' or a 'fragment'. In a series or a collection, photos establish contact with one another. EVERY PHOTO THAT EXISTS LEADS ITS OWN LIFE AT NIGHT.

❊ ❊ ❊

How light came into the world. Belated return of a fragment of Marx's writing. A classical source mentions that the term candela simplex, the 'simple' candle, first appears in the fifth century before Christ. It is believed that this candela was 'simply' produced by dipping a *funale* (a piece of string, a thin cord made out of reeds, rushes, papyrus stalks, perhaps even stringy pieces of oakum) in tallow; a thread covered by a thin layer of tallow. Then the candela simplex would have been a small tallow candle for the poor, or a thread in a small bowl of liquid wax. In the second century, the wick, filum or LIGHT-THREAD emerged for the first time. This candela burnt down quickly and had to be constantly tended. Characteristic of the burning candle is the BURN BOWL which is filled with liquid fuel and from which the end of the candle wick protrudes, bearing the flame. The burn bowl must therefore be sufficiently wide in relation to the length of the wick, and the fuel must be made of a distinct substance.

If a burn bowl can't be constructed, perhaps because both wick and fuel burn down together at the same speed (cord-like material, soaked in fuel), then the object in question is a 'torch'. Rather than a 'candle'. Why did the TORCH become the symbol of freedom instead of the CANDLE? The candle, the light of life, the symbol of mourning, but the torch a symbol of bombast, the symbol for those arriving at the Manhattan wharves?

These were questions discussed in a hitherto unknown text by Karl Marx, which was delivered to the cultural department of the Central Committee of East Germany's ruling Socialist Unity Party on 4 December 1989. The title of the fragment was 'Sacred material (materia sacra)'. The manuscript was bought at an auction by the East German agent Lieutenant David M. Frankfurter (in central England in October 1989).

✷ ✷ ✷

Sacred material (materia sacra): 'After the world was struck by a terrible calamity, the gods, men and animals all wept. Even the sun god Re wept. Tears fell from his eyes to the earth. They were transformed into a bee. The bee is a worker. Its work is to be found in flowers and trees. This is how wax and honey originates from the tears of the god Re.'

It goes on: 'Wax as a virginal product of the chaste bee.'

The bee: 'It ranks above all other animals. Though small of body, it bears in its breast a powerful spirit. It is weak in physical strength but strong in ingenuity. The female of the species is injured by no mate nor troubled by any offspring.'

The 'moist, waxy substance' possesses a sweet scent and a bright lustre. Technical comment: 'The candle is put together from three admirable components: (1) the nutrients from river plants (papyrus wick), (2) the substance provided by the unsullied and productive bee and (3) the fire poured down from the heavens (oxygen, breath). Unsullied by animal fat. We cut out the hidden religious allusions and are left with a political allegory.' (In places, the manuscript is difficult to read.)

Lieutenant Frankfurter and his colleague Fritzsche had delivered the document, which they had purchased at an auction for only 180 pounds, to the secretary of culture, a former émigré and sceptic, who, in view of the fact that the party conference already under way would lead to the dissolution of East Germany's ruling party, could no longer see any practical use for it. However, a young journalist from the *Berliner Zeitung* was still lurking around the halls of the Central Committee, hungry for news. He was under the impression that what would later come to be known as the *Wende*, or 'change', had already supplied him with the drug known as PUBLICITY. In those days, discipline in keeping secrets was no longer strict. Thus it was that the journalist A. Osang and Lieutenant D. Frankfurter, who had never met before, sat down opposite each other in the canteen.

OSANG. It's odd that this text contains no observations by the author making fun of such words as 'chastity', 'unsullied by man', 'virginal', 'admirable', 'unsullied and productive'. He wouldn't normally have missed that.

FRANKFURTER. He must have been in a serious mood.

OSANG. And you consider the text to be authentic?

FRANKFURTER. Beyond the shadow of a doubt. We examined the paper—it has a watermark that was only used up until 1858.

OSANG. But why was he so interested in the difference between a torch and a candle? Should a political movement charge forward under the 'torch of freedom' or the 'candle of patience'?

FRANKFURTER. The latter. The torch has been tried. The candle hasn't.

OSANG. Does the torch burn too quickly? Is that what our secret services came to realize?

FRANKFURTER. In reality everything takes longer.

OSANG. Do you think we might have won with a bit more bee-like diligence?

FRANKFURTER. The bee is an idol of bourgeois industriousness.

OSANG. Do you think we might have won as a bourgeois revolution?

FRANKFURTER. We might have been able to complete it, as a republic of the sons of the bourgeoisie.

OSANG. Have we ever seen a bourgeois revolution carried through to its end? In the manner of a candle, so to speak?

FRANKFURTER. It almost happened in Portugal.

OSANG. Too late for our republic?

FRANKFURTER. Probably.

OSANG. Are you sure?

FRANKFURTER. When the Central Committee isn't even excited about a newly discovered fragment from Marx's manuscripts.

OSANG. So was one of Marx's suggestions to replace the fortieth party conference's fast-burning torch with the 2,000-year-old patiently burning wax candle?

FRANKFURTER. That's why we brought the text all the way back here.

OSANG. Did you at least get your expenses paid?

FRANKFURTER. Not even our travel costs.

Between them the two men had downed seven schnapps. The view from the window revealed a world in twilight, indistinct and therefore full of hope.

❊ ❊ ❊

The human face is controlled by 200 elements, 26 of them muscles. Most of these elements cannot be consciously controlled. Conjuring up a facial expression out of this self-regulating flow is an art, one that can only be kept up for short periods of time.

If you fix these movements with Sellotape, it becomes evident that what we have beneath the forehead on the front side of our heads is not a 'face' but a kaleidoscope. Thus by sticking Sellotape to it one ordinary Monday morning in 1966 (as part of an artistic action), an actor's face became that of a forced labourer from 1944, a cardinal from 1492 or an actor at the Weimar Theatre from 1799. The Sellotape is not a disguise but, rather, a way of revealing the 'wave structure of the face' by suddenly stopping something that is everywhere and constantly in motion.

Indeed, FACE as such is a misleading term, in that the organ of smell, the orifice of the mouth, the ears on either side of the face and the open fields of the cheeks are in constant competition with the eyes. Several of the muscles that poker players need to control the current flowing across

their face are positioned in the middle of the skull. They originate in a column of muscles (an ancestor of the Tower of Babel) that formed a protective helmet of anger and enjoyment in both our closest animal relatives and the early hominids, and which completely controlled the animal's (or later biped's) countenance. It was a matter of linear strength and not play. It would not yet have been possible to speak of the 'play of expressions'.

✱ ✱ ✱

Silver content and grey tones: during the year 1966, it became known that the film company Ilford was about to greatly reduce the amount of silver in their 35mm black-and-white film stock. We bought large quantities of this negative, which was still available in 60- and 120-metre cans, and stored it in stacks it at the Institute for Film Production in Ulm and my production house in Munich. In this way, we stockpiled as much as we could get of a film stock that captured light so vividly.

The stock captures every distinction of light. Several Arriflex lenses, whose history goes back 400 years (to the Dutch lens grinders who developed the prototypes), focus light in the middle of the image, with the result that the grey tones run off from there to its edges. And what a wealth of grey tones! Nothing that Ilford produced in subsequent years could achieve the same effect. Since the eye would have to filter light itself out of the lava of colours, it is not visible to the idle attention of the ordinary gaze. It only becomes apparent when shown through a projector, namely, as LIGHT, BLACKS and GREYS.

It was the view of our cameraman Thomas Mauch that somewhere in the image there had to be black, somewhere there had to be white, and between these a tumult of grey tones could run riot. He was known as a collector of grey tones. In certain borderline light situations, for example

over several evenings in December 1965, he captured whole cascades of such tones which he felt should be edited into sequences that completely ignored the action of the film. It was these that seemed to him to be film's authentic messages, in contrast to its scripted scenes populated by mediocre actors. In terms of the actors' quality, action, facial expressions, intonation, individual appearance and talent for disguise, he could distinguish up to 60 differences per hour of shooting (out of 660 impressions that for him were just repetitions of things that had already been seen and that therefore could be ignored). By contrast, when it came to grey tones he could observe over the same period of time (partly because the light conditions became increasingly favourable as the afternoon advanced) 7,800 differences, among them over seven singularities that he had never seen before, and which he believed had never even been filmed before. This cameraman was known for his quick eye. The chief film editor (who also had a sensitive nature, though for other things than this) later mixed these discoveries up and even let some of them disappear into the remainder material (the remainders not used in the film were packed into cans and at some point spoilt in the copying plant's cellars, since the chemical does not stop reacting and in the end destroys itself).

Mauch often had to be reminded to point the camera back at the action, because he had turned away from the set to film grey-tone phenomena. At that time, we shot every scene just *once* — which is not usual in the film industry — partly out of superstition and partly to keep ourselves in a state of creative tension. If every scene that goes wrong can be reshot, and if the film doesn't get into a crisis during editing, then it gets fat and intervenes between the viewer and the living impetus that we (there were 17 of us on set) felt during filming.

✿ ✿ ✿

The killer survived the night of the murders of 13 to 14 July 1966, in which he killed eight student nurses from Chicago, by 25 years. The news of these murders went around the world. Skilful and intensive profiling has meant that a great deal is known about what went on in the murderer's mind that night; what the eight student nurses from the hall of residence in Chicago might have felt while under his power is not known. The killer told the police that he had raped only his last victim, certainly not all of them. He tortured his victims for about an hour each, each one in a different room. He said he had had it in mind to 'kill each of the women he'd tied up in a particular way'. It became evident, however, that the murders had been carried out schematically. In his hurry, he found he couldn't come up with any ideas. One of the nurses bit him. The wound hurt; it was this wound that later betrayed him. He lost control. He barely noticed a single material fact from that night.

Apart from the eight nurses who were killed, there was, however, a ninth. She had (like the goat in the fairy tale who hides from the wolf inside the grandfather clock) crawled under a bed. His interrogator John Douglas reported that the killer had noticed her trying to save her life but had then forgotten this ninth victim. This when one of the main motivations the murderer later spoke of was to leave no one alive who might later be able to identify him. This single 'rational'

reason for his actions (among so many irrational ones which were harder to formulate) had become muddled during the course of the extravagant and (considered as the work of a single night) inflationary events. He realized too late that there was one crime he had forgotten to commit. It seemed inadvisable to him to go back, since he assumed that someone had already raised the alarm.

Then, at a medical station where he had gone to have his throbbing bite wound treated, he was recognized by his tattoo which the ninth nurse had described. He was arrested as he left the station. Thus the two nurses, each in a different way, had been able to avenge the murders. The ninth nurse, the one who had been spared, remained single for a long time. It seemed that no one had the courage to come near the spurned victim. The aura of murder hung too closely around her.

In the UNREAL DREAM OF THAT NIGHT, the senses lose hold on reality. A young man from the suburbs of Chicago, who had briefly got to know the ninth nurse and had then, once he'd heard who she was, quickly backed off, stated that he'd thought of her as a murderer who could do him some kind of harm, despite the fact that this man was considerably physically stronger than the nurse, whose slight build had enabled her to crawl under the low-lying bedstead with such ease. He was in control of the situation but not in control of his imagination.

❊ ❊ ❊

An unknown composition by Luigi Nono from 1966: Seventy of the waiters who went down with the Titanic in 1912 came from neighbouring villages in the Abruzzi. Not one of their fiancées, who had hoped that these men would return home and marry them once they'd been paid their wages, ever found anyone else who would. The villages remained childless, and today stand desolate among the mountains. It was to these VOICELESS PEOPLE OF HISTORY that

Nono dedicated his *Lament for Twelve Strings and Twelve Sopranos* in 1966. The grief is not so much for the waiters lost at the bottom of the sea as it is for the miserable fate of the women left behind, who were forbidden by strict local custom from seeking another husband in a neighbouring town.

❖ ❖ ❖

The Red Guards travelled across China's vast expanses, exploring in trucks and on foot all that was now theirs: the whole of their world, the whole of society. From Shanghai, that immense landscape of communes and factories, delegations set off for the provinces. It was vital that the reactionary forces not be left any time to organize and strike back. Groups of civil war veterans (17 years had passed since the victory of the revolution) were making contact with one another, seeking one another's support for protection from exposure as counter-revolutionaries. In May 1966, civil war could have broken out—or an utterly new way of life. Now would have been the right moment for the calm theoretical research work that had lent the movement a sense of direction: 'There is no practice without theory.'

At the same time, the picture GIRL RIDING ON A DONKEY appeared in Europe—under the same stars and constellations of the celestial powers that governed the movement in the Far East. In the picture, the donkey gazed amiably at the viewer. So did the girl riding him. Her expression was in a certain sense both 'foolish' and 'full of expectation'.

The archetype for this image was that armed and mounted girl of antiquity who had been driven mad by her love for Achilles. One of her descendants was to be found in one of the last films to premiere in the Third Reich, namely, *Opfergang* (*Rite of Sacrifice*): in it, she appears as a young woman from 1939, dressed in an animal skin, armed with a bow and arrow, and dashing along the beach on a white racehorse, who catches the eye of Carl Raddatz, the gentlemanly equestrian whom she proceeds to entrap and lead astray. In his film *Mutters Maske* (Mother's Mask), Christoph Schlingensief captured on celluloid this RECUR-RING STORY of a 'woman on a horse' (while centaurs are teachers, women who are half-horse are seductresses) as a word-for-word remake of *Opfergang*. In it, a plump, young inhabitant of Mühlheim rides a pony. She has her attack dogs with her, which she could set on her lover to tear out his throat.

※ ※ ※

Just as the first reports of the Cultural Revolution were coming out of the People's Republic of China, Carl Schmitt, an enthusiast for all things new, received at his home in Plettenberg a delegation of French students from the Sorbonne 'with great excitement'. Though a remote region of the planet in European terms, things had been brewing in Plettenberg since 1965, just as they had in Berkeley. The conversation, in French and German, went on late into the afternoon. Was the entire world undergoing a period of renewal (just as it had during the axial period 500 years before Christ)? The influence of a black spirit sun was, he claimed, causing upheaval, just as in certain periods a doppelgänger star had frequently set the solar system and

all its heavenly bodies trembling. Schmitt had often added to his collection of presentiments the signs of a GLOBAL NEW AGE, but had repeatedly been disappointed.

In November 1966, the government of Chancellor Erhard fell. On 1 December, the new men of the Grand Coalition took up office — there were new faces but no new age. From then until the end of the year, there was no hope of the radical change he'd been waiting for. Carl Schmitt: always in expectant readiness, prepared for any surprise — novarum rerum cupidus.

❊ ❊ ❊

The art of premonition. In an attic room near Bielefeld, unnoticed by the West German public but in contact with her followers through a monthly newsletter, lived the once-famous clairvoyant and medium Elise Kelpe.

Using her sensitive nerves, she would feel out through the window, 'divining' the world outside, seeking to learn something of the details of the year 1966 so she could write about it in her December newsletter. Like most other people, all that she knew about what was going on in the world came through news reports. What is there that was real about the 'premonition of the world', as Elise was able to sense it in her attic near Bielefeld, above all at twilight? What did the 'bloodless coup by Argentinian generals' that the radio reported mean to Kelpe? I see blood on these hands, Mrs Kelpe remarked, who in the course of her long life had often read similar announcements relating to events in other parts of the world, and knew their outcome. She knew it before the persecutions in southern Latin America had even begun. Regarding the Cultural Revolution and certain events in Africa, she observed: If a revolution had happened there, I'd have felt it in my solar plexus. She often listened to music on Westdeutscher Rundfunk, a popular radio station. Then, borne aloft by the music, she was able to 'feel ahead' from the year 1966 to 2066. There were rents and tears in reality. They needed to be sewn together. In her newsletter, Mrs Kelpe warned against any cheerful faces at New Year's Eve.

✳ ✳ ✳

Newspapers and their pictures remain responsible for our knowledge of what is happening in reality. Very little of this can be checked using our own senses. However, without such news, the world we immediately perceive around us would have no collective rhythm. Indirect experience, such as the view of things from a distance, is unreal. But proximity is, in its own way, equally unreal. Would I, for example, be real here? Then again, I may be talking to someone and notice myself making an impatient gesture that I recognize as being my mother's. It has crept into my movements. Such movements from earlier times (caused by individuals who are not in the room, in other words, by the anchor of the past) constitute a choir which reacts to the events of the moment. I carry them with me throughout the day, whether or not I notice it. In the end, these stones that I stumble over are a means of understanding why I'm in such a hurry to get to where I'm going right now in Frankfurt's Monday morning traffic.

What actually happens when you fall out of reality? This question was put to a former female bishop of the Evangelical Church in Germany. You cannot fall out of God's hand, was her succinct reply.

It wasn't easy explaining to a theological layman from the daily press exactly what a 'reality that you cannot fall out of' is. It's a second skin, a third dress or a house people live in that doesn't look like a house. If this house called reality collapses, the bishop went on, or if it is bombed or burns down, then we need to build a new one.

But you can't do that with your skin, replied the journalist, who seemed actually to be more sympathetic than she had first thought. We can't shed our skin like reptiles. And that's why there's a way of falling out of reality that nothing can make up for. You mean, asked the theologian, like when your skin is literally flayed, as in a medieval torture? The martyrs of antiquity also had to suffer that.

The conversation then went on the whole night. If, for example, essential parts of a person are caught in the reality that is lost, his soul, and with it sometimes also his body, is torn. Or, added the journalist, the tear in the soul deprives the body of meaning. You can put it either way, replied the theologian. And there are instances when God has to take the person who has been TORN BY FALLING OUT OF REALITY unto Himself. Each of them had drunk a large number of beers, found that they liked each other and were suffering no kind of despair themselves.

✳ ✳ ✳

Eulenspiegel inside the horse's skin. Despite having been sentenced to death under the laws of the land, Eulenspiegel returned and was travelling through the country when he saw the prince's henchmen approaching from afar. He slaughtered his horse, pulled out its entrails and crept inside its skin, sewing it shut behind him. Confronted with this peculiar structure, the prince's chamberlain was wondering what to tell the henchmen to do, when Eulenspiegel called to him from the safety of his hiding place: he was not, he said, in the land of the prince but, rather, in his own land. Or did the chamberlain doubt that the horse was his own? The irreality of the situation struck the chamberlain, and later also the prince, when the incident was related to him. The ruler was not certain how his people would react if he continued to pursue Eulenspiegel, who was clearly separated from the reality of his country by the horse's skin. So he invited Eulenspeigel to come out, having assured him of safe conduct out of his realm.

5

The gradual ebbing of the mind's acuity in old age. At critical moments in the Seven Years' War, King Frederick II of Prussia was known for taking in the essential elements of a battlefield in a *single* glance and using this as the basis for unexpected decisions. His senses and his brain, which shaped the world around him, organized the conditions for this almost automatically. They lent the king his intuition, his sharply defined 'insight', his ability to quickly plot a piece of land and its obstacles (such as ditches, small rivers or marshes), but also his capacity to judge the enemy's spirit, which he determined from the manner in which its columns marched towards him (sluggishly or vigorously). In this way, he cast, in the manner of a language, a central perspective over a world of possible events. The prince's gift for rapidly grasping a situation could—such as when he spoke French, or misunderstood German when spoken by several different people all at once—cause him to jump to freakish and misguided conclusions, as it did in the case of the terrible defeat at Kunersdorf.

Now, however, in his old age, this capacity for 'rapidly surmising a situation' had left him. His mind could only slowly bring itself to do even the preliminary work. His impressions became blurred. In the so-called Potato War against Bavaria, he no longer wanted to direct the battles himself. He often, while trying to complete his observations, forgot his initial impressions. This slow ebbing of the spirit, this forgetfulness, also diminished his awareness of the situation around him. There was no one in his circle who was either qualified or authorized to confront him with the condition in which he found himself.

❊ ❊ ❊

He tries calling his son. No answer. A period of waiting. Then his daughter, and then his wife. They can't be reached on their mobile phones. A pause in his life. He can still feel the urgency of the day's demands in his body but he has no one he can talk to.

The view from the window shows a group of trees, dark green in the evening light. There is still light in their topmost branches, the last parting traces of the day. On a tea trolley (two generations older than its observer) a glass candlestick supports four candles whose colours vary between blue and pale violet, depending on the light coming from the window. If the waiting man were to die soon, it would continue to stand there for a while; since there was never any reason for putting it by the window in the first place, there is also scarcely any reason for moving it. The evenings I have yet to see are numbered. Most will pass without my noticing the gradual fading of the light, because I won't be having to wait, I will be in the company of others, or I will be busy and will be able to reach the people I love. So this short sequence of minutes is, perhaps, a unique period of time before the speeches that will be held at the end.

The colour of life outside the window has already changed. The light illuminating the edges of the trees has gone. The unused candles have lost their blue and violet colours. Right in front of me a collection of pencils and two sharpeners stand next to a lamp which will soon be switched on. There's a lot to do. Now I have to get something to eat.

❊ ❊ ❊

While setting up a business account to manage a property he'd bought in Berlin during the real estate boom of the 1990s, a wealthy businessman was required by a large foreign bank to prove his identity. The requirement was part of the regulations on money laundering. He had to visit a branch of this bank in a large west German city, taking with him his passport and accompanied by his wife (who was joint owner of the property and who also had to bring her passport with her). There they waited in line at a respectful distance from the counter. When his turn came, the bank clerk contacted the bank's Berlin branch only to discover that, like many businesses in the capital, it did not open until later in the day. The man was told he would have to wait.

The businessman was not used to spending a substantial part of his Monday morning waiting.

The couple drank an espresso at a nearby cafe. After returning to the bank, they found that there was still something else that needed to be cleared up. Their passports were still being held.

This is an example of the dividing line between a system, in this case a large bank, and the rest of the world. Had he been a customer of the bank himself, and therefore inside the system, the busy and influential businessman would have been very obligingly treated. He wouldn't have wasted any time. But since he was dealing with a foreign bank, one to which he was an outsider (who had literally come in from the street), and with which he'd already lodged a heated complaint, thus reinforcing the distance between outside and inside, the external barriers were difficult to overcome. It would, he said to his wife, be unimaginable for a traveller in one of Schubert's *Lieder* to walk through a town, go into a bank and find himself subject to some kind of regulation regarding an object he had with him, something valuable, for example. Banks are not as interested in attracting customers as they used to be. Since he'd made a formal complaint, and since a representative from the bank's central branch, which was located in another part of the city, had to be called to receive this complaint, it wasn't until midday

that the identification process was over. The irritation he felt
exacerbated his high blood pressure.

✳ ✳ ✳

The composer Karlheinz Stockhausen, who composed his
series *Moments* between 1962 and 1969 and later wrote the
work SATURDAY FROM LIGHT, defined his concept of
the MOMENT FORM as 'AN ETERNITY THAT DOES
NOT BEGIN AT THE END OF TIME BUT WHICH IS
ATTAINABLE AT EVERY MOMENT'. 'Depending on

their characteristics, moments can be as long or as short as one likes', he added. In so doing, he referred to a dispute he once claimed to have had with Werner Heisenberg (when he was staying at the Siemens studio for electronic music in Munich). And it may be he misunderstood him, at least to the effect that—in the same way that at the level of Planck space the beginning of the world repeats itself in every temporal interval of now-time, in other words, the universe renews and produces itself at the elementary level from one second to the next while still possessing a beginning and a distant future, as far, that is, as light has been able to travel, meaning that all things have a life in duration and a life in the moment—everything that can enter into the sounds of a piece of music always does so in a two-fold manner: as a now and as a duration, as a punctum and as an entire piece.

—Can a sound also be rooted in both?

—No.

—Why not?

—Because our access to the moment and our access to the end of the world belong to two different worlds.

—Parallel worlds?

—Antiworlds!

❅ ❅ ❅

In the last year of his life, Christoph Schlingensief, who was being bombarded with offers and whom the director of the Bavarian State Opera had asked to direct *Tristan* as his next but one project, began planning a production of Wagner's *Ring Cycle*. He was only prepared to take on the staging the work if he was allowed to perform the sequence of its operas in reverse order: beginning with the TWILIGHT OF THE GODS, then SIEGFRIED, then the VALKYRIE and finally the RHEINGOLD. At the end, however (since the RHEINGOLD is short), 'dreamlike' renditions of the TODESVERKÜNDIGUNG from the VALKYRIE and

SIEGFRIED'S DEATH from the TWILIGHT OF THE GODS would be repeated as concertantes. And really SIEGFRIED'S DEATH should be heard first, and only then the TODES-VERKÜNDIGUNG. The ending should be composed of a moment of great anticipation and complete openness of action. He was convinced that this sequence—in sensory terms, utterly satisfying—would become the established one for Wagner's *Ring*. The waves of the Rhine, which overflow their banks in the third act of the TWILIGHT OF THE GODS, and the scene of Valhalla in flames should visually transform themselves into the star masses of a galaxy, so that it becomes clear that

Wagner is not only describing the drama of a race of gods and their great fall from power but that this work is also about the history of time on earth, namely, 4.5 billion years, which moves backwards as well as forwards, and which is not an arrow but a circle, and which, like the serpent, inhabits Mount Kailash. Wagner was definitely a Buddhist, and merely concealed this in a private religion decked out with the trappings of Christianity. Schlingensief was in a hurry. He sensed that his body was in revolt. He was counting his days.

❋ ❋ ❋

He changed his name repeatedly. He experimented with names. His mother left him when he was a year old, something he hadn't been consciously aware of. Later, after he had become a famous PUBLIC FIGURE (in possession of no substantial personal fortune, but it *seemed* as if he must have had some money), this ruthless mother returned and legally confiscated a third of his income as her maintenance.

There had always been rumours. Had the husband of this selfish mother, the genius' father, been a Jew? Or had his father been a Hungarian cavalry officer? The actor, critic, cabaret performer and scholar Egon F. possessed a degree of corpulence that bore no relation to his father's skeletal frame or to his energetic mother's spindly body. He remained tall in stature, and no night, no amount of boozing, no change of profession (from writing about mysterious connections going back over 6,000 years to being applauded at his well-paid public appearances) could unsettle him. An indescribably crisis-resistant body which was inhabited by more than 88 different spirits.

A piece of meat leaps from a windowsill. He saw the SA men approaching the building. He heard the concierge speaking to the men outside. He had stayed too long in Vienna. The fact is that he hadn't thought it possible they'd want to kill him — him, the son of a Hungarian hussar (and if he'd made public this fact early enough, he might not have been classified as a half-Jew). His political convictions lay 'to the right of the National Socialists' but partly also to the extreme left of them. They could have learnt from him.

He set aside his doubts. Once he'd opened the windows overlooking the street, he was able to get up and balance on the windowsill. It meant he couldn't simply fall once he'd taken the monstrous decision but had to make it a second time. He called down to the passers-by in the street: Look out! At this point there was no trace of the National Socialists down there; they were still conferring at the door of the apartment house. The decision to jump comes unconsciously—it is, in fact, not a decision. What else could he

have done? Three people had sent him out into the world: the selfish mother, the borrowed stepfather and an anonymous cavalry officer. The difference among them had made him mistrustful (him, the success story of all Vienna's nights). For the first time, the consequences of this mistrust, unanchored in his body, are directly felt. He jumps without thinking. His assumptions that the National Socialists would be either tolerant or blind, assumptions that had caused him to remain in Vienna too long, had been false.

❀ ❀ ❀

The designer Horst Sachtleben does not consider the centipede to make a very attractive emblem. On the other hand, emblems such as dolphins, eagles and lions are overused. The sociologist Gerda Hildebrandt replied that the centipede's qualities would make it a suitable symbol for intelligence or technology, given that it's no longer in control of its own feet and is constantly pushing forward. The animal is also considered to be agile.

—It's transparent and flat.

—Unpleasant to touch.

—On the other hand, lions (being meateaters) generally have stinking jaws.

—You don't see that on an emblem.

—Centipedes look like woodlice. No one wants them in their kitchen.

—You could say the same of eagles. Would you hang an eagle's claw gripping the remains of a sheep on your wall? That would be disgusting.

Sachtleben concluded that emblems come into being when the qualities of the thing they represent are collectively and tacitly forgotten, enabling them to refer to only part of what is known about them. It is this, says Gerda Hildebrandt, that explains why it is so difficult to develop new emblems for the new qualities emerging in human beings. Centipedes are active in and around them. What people do in the twenty-first century, and what the technology they've created presents them with, cannot be associated with the image of a lion, who feeds on carrion.

❊ ❊ ❊

The works of Mao Zedong, secluded behind glass. In the bare office room that had been allocated to Theodor W. Adorno in the Institute for Social Research's Senckenberg building—which effectively turned into an imaginary room when he was dictating his notes from the previous day to his secretary Elfriede Olbach—stood a glass cabinet. The guidelines laid down by the construction office of the state of Hessen's finance department had determined that an item of furniture of this kind, designed to contain books, should be part of the office furnishings for all directors and vice-directors of academic institutions. The glass doors of the cabinet ensured that the books remained enclosed but visible. Adorno did not keep any of his own books in this dictating room. The cabinet contained only Mao Zedong's *Collected Works* which had been sent to the Institute the year before by the embassy of the People's Republic. The yellow case-bound volumes remained where they were, arranged in order and unread, until his death. Taking the books home with him seemed unwarranted to the philosopher, as well as unseemly (they were also a heavy load to carry). He found it equally hard to give the books away (to whom?) or to leave them out for people to take.

❖ ❖ ❖

The same winter that Barbara Tuchman's *August 1914* appeared on the West German book market, I brought a copy with me to Halberstadt for my father, so he would have plenty to read in the darkening afternoons when his surgery was closed. He rationed out the text into daily portions, refraining, despite his curiosity, from devouring the precious item too quickly. He read the book several times. As he did, he started noting down on his prescription pads his own impressions of those first days of war (partly reminiscences, partly passages collected from various sources, including documents other than Tuchman's book). He started cutting pictures out of books and sticking them into a notebook, selecting pages into which he later inserted the observations of the 22-year-old he had been back in August 1914. On the day after he was called up, the NCOs received the recruits in Berlin and lined them up in order of height. My father's diminutive stature would normally have meant that he would have been excluded from the ranks of the grenadier guards and transferred to another, less distinguished regiment, had not the recruits' good-humoured training sergeant, who was able to order a preliminary medical examination, assigned him the post of medical orderly and candidate for the position of junior doctor in a field hospital attached to the Guards' regiment. In this unit his short height would be less of an obstacle, since it did not take part in parades.

The train journeys west, the long periods of waiting at the junctions where freight traffic would build up, the approach to the front—all this he found described in Tuchman's book or guessed it by reading between the lines. But there was also the wider overview of events which none of the participants could have had at the time—the military gossip among sections of the general staff and the judgements passed on each other by von Kluck and von Bülow, the commanders in chief of the First and the Second Armies. Then there was the commander of the Third Army—a Saxon bourgeois obsessed with success yet a procrastinator, a cunctator. All this could be relived. North of Paris, two army corps under General Colonel von Kluck and his chief of staff von Kuhl had almost won the victory that would have enabled them to occupy the French capital.

He had 'experienced' all the things that Tuchman described as they happened, assiduously working in the field hospital, a lowly medical orderly and not yet a doctor. He had cleaned bowls and vessels, made and unmade beds, received deliveries of freshly wounded soldiers and hurriedly carried messages between the doctors and leading medical experts. In fact he'd seen nothing of what Tuchman described. He'd 'experienced' it subsequently, when reports trickled down from above, and when higher-ranking 'colleagues' discussed the situation among themselves. One experiences what one is told.

With his gaze firmly averted from the present (characterized by the municipality of Magdeburg's dreadful winter management of the town, which left streets uncleared of snow and water frozen in pipes), my father reconstructed the days leading up to December 1914, critical times, because so much could have turned out differently to the way it did. A historical alternative to the Battle of the Marne, for example, which might have led to a negotiated peace on Christmas Eve 1914, would not have been advantageous to the course of my father's life. Had Germany won, he would have had to spend the rest of his life working off the costs of his studies as an army doctor at the Pépinière, the military medical school in Berlin, something the defeat of 1918 meant he didn't have to do. Reading Tuchman's book made him want to start writing himself. He decided the book would take the form of a diary. He had the manuscript bound in the lower town in a simple leather cover, and tied it round with a piece of string that held the volume together. This was his second attempt at writing a book. His first book was a kind of lexicon in which he recorded entries for all the more unusual diseases that he knew. For the more common diseases, by contrast, he had prepared lists and commentaries describing their different varieties. Thus *one* particular case of bronchitis is not like *another*. Rather, it is a question of distinguishing among the 88 different ways that coughs and afflictions of the trachea and the bronchial tubes can develop. Only four of these were apt to produce a lung infection. Still more varied is the medical and zoological garden of jaundice, new cases of which appear every Christmas, which would otherwise only be encountered during jaundice epidemics, after country weddings or intensive drinking bouts. According to his notes, the disease can develop in 126 different ways, and it was an illness he had a special affinity for, because he him-self had suffered more than one serious case of jaundice. He recognized jaundice as soon as the patient walked into his consulting room.

❊ ❊ ❊

Departure for war (Le Départ pour la Guerre). An open fire. A cat has been warming itself next to it. The grandmother is handing the soldier—the latter in boots, red trousers, ammu-nition belt, and rifle in hand—a baby in nappies. The father looks disapprovingly at his daughter, a young peasant woman squatting at the table in her galoshes, who, perturbed by the prospect of war, weeps uncontrollably. The bowls the four of them had been sipping coffee from just hours before are standing, cleared to one side, on the table.

✳ ✳ ✳

In 1940, six horse-drawn carts crossed France's country roads to reach the outskirts of Paris. They had with them exhibits belonging to a small museum in a provincial town near Amiens, which were being moved to safety against the

German advance. Junk. They included several oil paintings showing scenes from the war of 1870–71 but also a papier mâché model of an entire trench from the 1914 war, as well as portraits in reproduction of all of Napoleon's marshals. The carts reached the centre of Paris just in time, that is, before the German troops were able to overtake them. They made their way to Les Halles, the neighbourhood of Paris now dominated by the Pompidou Centre. Assuming that the paintings would not appeal to the German occupiers, their keepers, having found refuge in Paris, placed them with their faces to the wall. This is how the small museum's inventory was stored, stacked in sheds easily accessible

through the building's courtyard, until the occupiers withdrew a few years later. The forgotten exhibits are still waiting to be brought home.

❊ ❊ ❊

Quote from the Pseudo-Hippocrates (Neoplatonic-Arabic): According to Aristotle, FORM (Being), that is, the GOD OF PURE THOUGHT, is the Prime Mover and entirely devoid of all matter.

This remark troubled the doctors of Alexandria. Their actual observation of the difference between life and death (when a human being or even an animal died) contradicted the logical division between existence and essence, since they believed they could always observe an 'oscillation', and in many cases a doctor would succeed in kindling a low-burning candle back to full life, restoring one Greek ruler to another 21 years of life beyond the death Aristotelean logic had ordained for him.

Out of God's pure Being emanates pure intellect (or spirit), which, however, in contrast to the pure BEING OF GOD, already contains the Many. And this real spirit also emanates further into the material world in which we live. Nevertheless, intelligible nature is existent as a whole and moreover as an ENTELECHY DOWN TO ITS LAST DETAIL, as that which the doctor sees in the sick or healthy organism—always twofold and therefore graspable (as a shadow) by the doctor.

❊ ❊ ❊

A shallow lake, formed by a dam. A water installation covering a broad stone slab, and incorporating a rectangular erratic block which stands in front of the grand hotel. You cannot see where the floor of the lake begins to shelve away; it is hidden beneath clear, tempting water that seems to have no bottom. A child is stumbling through the shallow summer water towards the edge of the artwork. On either side of him two guardian angels are waiting, his mother and his father. They catch the child as he reaches the edge of the lake, at the point where the fun to be had in splashing through the element crosses its limit and the deep water begins. The child immediately turns back and runs through the shallow water to the other side, where its other parent it is waiting for it just where the water becomes dangerous.

❊ ❊ ❊

I'm walking with my sister in the mountains. Two riders approach us on a steep mountain path. The adult horses are followed at some distance by a foal. We greet the rider and his daughter, and watch the fine horses as they go past; then we are appalled when the foal suddenly gallops along the

steep, grassy slope to the right of us, right along the edge of the precipice where a single misplaced step would cause the animal to lose its balance. The foal didn't want to run into us.

Distracted by the adult riders, we were blocking the middle of the path. But the young animal, reluctant to follow behind the slow-moving horses, and wishing (spurred by some impulse) to overtake us all, bolted ahead towards the most dangerous part of the path. These flight animals have an instinctive sense of the obstacles and pitfalls around them. Just as other animals feel protected by their acute sense of smell. Or just as human beings deny the existence of a danger by retreating into an imaginary world — an instinct that is, however, never as useful as the one possessed by flight animals who blaze an escape route along the edge of the abyss.

❊ ❊ ❊

Path through the dark forest. During his lifetime, Karl Emmecke found his daily walk through the shale-strewn wood along the side of the mountain blocked by roadworks. The East German authorities' habitual neglect meant that for a long time the road remained so rudimentary that he could easily cross it. This changed once funds started arriving from the west after 1991, when a waist-high metal barrier was built and a ditch dug along the side of the road. Emmecke now found that, in the middle of his life, the walk he was so fond of had been severely curtailed. He hopes this isn't a sign that his life is also going to be curtailed. When it comes to the 'path through the dark forest', Emmecke is not much good at adapting.

❊ ❊ ❊

After a day full of telephone calls and stress, he found he could no longer follow the thriller by John Grisham as he sat reading it on the lavatory that evening.

It was about a delinquent by the name of Raymond. The weary reader was unable to distinguish him from the story's murder victim whose name was Childers. He had to keep leafing back through the pages. The novel had no list of names.

The days of our life, and the hours of our waking lives, are finite. Infinite, however, are the growing demands made by modern communications. They had left this CEO exhausted beyond measure. He hoped to keep going for another three months, when he might be able to take a holiday (consisting of one weekend and three week days). His high-ranking position placed him in a region of the social stratosphere where the oxygen was thin and the other living organisms few in number—there were too many worries, and too much time stolen; even during the shortest pauses in the day, someone was always picking away at the remnants of his attention like a bird of prey.

'"This was the day she prayed for," said Leon,' read the tired man. Who, though, were the characters in the novel? In the course of the day, he had had to draw many distinctions between characters and matters of fact, with the result that he had no desire to meet anyone new from the realm of fiction. He therefore set the book aside, and concentrated on digesting. This, like an indolent dog, calmly went on working beneath all his life's stress and impoverishment.

❆ ❆ ❆

The path leads through a ravine. A handrail has been put up so no one falls over the edge. It is already damaged. A photograph captures the moment before the hand grasps the rail. SOLID SUPPORT: REALITY.

Notes

1   A reference to the evacuation of German citizens from the country's
    former eastern territories as the Soviet armies advanced in 1944–45.

2   From the Epic of Gilgamesh, an ancient Mesopotamian epic poem
    about Gilgamesh, king of the Mesopotamian city-state of Uruk.

A.K.
born 14 February 1932

G.R.
born 9 February 1932

This collaboration between two artists—one working with text, the other images—has its origins in a number of chance meetings at the Hotel Waldhaus in Sils-Maria in the Engadine. After spending New Year's Eve of 2009 to 2010 there together, the idea came about of cooperating on a work that incorporated both images and texts. That project, *December*, comprising 39 stories by Alexander Kluge and 39 pictures by Gerhard Richter, was published by Suhrkamp in the autumn of 2010—and also appeared in English and French translations. The present book, conceived after a meeting between Richter and Kluge in Berlin, takes up again the thread of their collaboration.